LOST GIRL

of the Lake

PRAISE FOR
LOST GIRL OF THE LAKE!

"*Lost Girl of the Lake* is just about perfect. A full-blown horror novel boiled down to novella length. It is concise, creepy and compulsively readable. I loved it."

–Bentley Little, Bram Stoker Winning author of *The Handyman*

"Joe McKinney and Michael McCarty write with one clear, poignant voice, weaving a narrative as haunting as it is nostalgic."

–David Dunwoody, author of *The Strange Dead*

"This story will draw you in just like the Lost Girl draws the story-teller—and like him, you'll be happy to go."

–Steve Englehart, author of *Marvel Masterworks: Captain America Vol. 9*

"*Lost Girl of the Lake* is an unconventional 'coming of age story' as only authors Joe McKinney and Michael McCarty could invent. It is an endearing, evocative saga filled with the familiar as well as the unexpected, infused with wonders of the heart and soul. A tale of dark seduction and innocence, told through a man's mind, recreated from his boyhood memory. I highly recommend this page turning novella and glimpse into both the past and future with unanswered mysteries lurking in the wings."

–Jody R. LaGreca, author of *Forever in Vein*

"McKinney and McCarty's *Lost Girl of the Lake* is a haunting coming-of-age story guaranteed to chill readers to the bone."

–Amy Grech, author of *Rage and Redemption in Alphabet City*

"In *Lost Girl of the Lake*, McCarty and McKinney have fashioned a vivid family remembrance of youth and days gone by that is both touching and terrifying."

–Bruce Boston, Bram Stoker winning author of *Resonance Dark & Light*

"Joe McKinney and Michael McCarty have spun a wonderful tale with *Lost Girl of the Lake*. They are wicked, lyrical and masterful as they paint a colorful picture of decades past and innocence lost. This novella is haunting, mysterious and seductive all at once. These two voices are wonderful and unforgettable. A must read for fans of modern dark fiction."

–Sandy DeLuca, author of *From Ashes*

LOST GIRL
of the Lake

Joe McKinney & Michael McCarty

Introduction
by
Gene O'Neill

A
Grinning Skull Press
Publication
P.O. Box 67, Bridgewater, MA 02324

DEDICATED TO

Clark Ashton Smith
H.P. Lovecraft
Robert R. McCammon
Stephen King

CONTENTS

ACKNOWLEDGMENTS

Michael would like to thank:

My blood brother Joe McKinney for letting me share in this adventure.

My lovely wife Cindy McCarty.

My good friend Mark McLaughlin for his great advice.

Grinning Skull Press, Michael Evans, Harrison Graves, Holly, Mel Piff, The Source Book Store, The Book Rack, Ron Stewart, Dave & Julie, Gene O'Neill, Chef Steph, Jo Ann Brown, Carma & Family, Brian Kronfeld, Quinn, Izzy, Andrew Murray, Hellnotes.com, Bad Moon Books, Don D'Ammassa, Latte, mom and to the pretty teenage girl back in the 1980s who wanted to go skinny dipping with me when I worked at the Bel-Air Drive-In (although we never did get to do that) and to my family and friends and fans everywhere.

Joe would like to thank:

Michael McCarty, my blood brother, for bringing me out of the woods.

My wife Tina, and our two lovely daughters, Elena and Brenna.

Joe and Jennifer McKinney, Clay and Tiffany McKinney, Mark Onspaugh, Tobey Crockett, Kevin and Crystal Luzius, Mark Kolodziejski, Arthur Casas, Michael Starnes,

Adam Zeldes, Matt Louis, David Snell, Brent Smith, Gene O'Neill, Bruce Boston, Marge Simon, Matt Staggs, Michelle Mondo, Steve Wedel, Gabrielle Faust, Joel Sutherland, Out of the Gutter Magazine, Mitchel Whitington, and all the wonderful men and women in the San Antonio Police Department. But a very special thanks to that being, power, force, whatever, that watched over me during those wild, troubled days of my youth. I owe you one. Several, actually.

Introduction to
Lost Girl of the Lake

Collaborations are difficult to keep in one voice. Often there are visible seams, with more than one voice noticeable. Although it may be low key, good readers find seams unsettling. Of course, the writers can *cheat* when there are two main characters. Each writes in the voice of only one character. Then, two voices are functional and relevant. And the collaboration works neatly. But sometimes, even when the two writers are highly gifted and work very carefully together, mixing their writing, a few visible seams creep into the narrative. Only the very best readers will notice, but this will be troubling to those readers. Not to worry with *Lost Girl of the Lake*; Joe McKinney and Michael McCarty are both highly skilled collaborators, working together seamlessly.

In a singular strong voice, reminiscent a bit of Stephen King writing at the top of his game, the two Macs develop a compelling coming-of-age story. And even though set in the 60s of hot, humid East Texas, not in King's Maine, the novella indeed reminds the reader of a coming-of-age tale *IT*, or perhaps more specifically, *The Body*.

The writing is precise and crisp, the plotting flawless, the sense of apprehension maintained at a disturbing electric level throughout. And like King's best work, *Lost Girl of the Lake* is wrapped up neatly, leaving no loose ends.

Plus…plus, that added grand touch that is guaranteed to scare the pants off of every living soul—*snakes*, lots and lots of clammy, writhing copperheads.

Do yourself a favor and pick up this excellent novella… You can thank me down the road.

–Gene O'Neill, *Lethal Birds* and
The Crime Files of Katy Green trilogy

"Childhood is a branch of cartography."

—Michael Chabon, "Manhood for Amateurs:
the Wilderness of Childhood"

Chapter One

I don't even remember the name of the road we took to get there. I've been struggling with that little detail for the last couple of days, trying to remember, trying to get started. But I've come to the conclusion that some details just don't matter. Not in the way it counts, anyway. I close my eyes and I picture this rambling country road cutting through a dense East Texas pine forest that stretches endlessly up to the sky. The name of the road is not important now. It's nothing but a number on an out-of-date map anyway. Like the pine forests that once surrounded it, it's a ghost of the past, just another fossil of my youth drowned deep beneath the brown waters of Lake Livingston.

For days now I have been trying to get at a boy's story with the learned software of a man's mind, and that's a mistake. The man and the boy don't speak the same language anymore; the road between them has been washed away. The man wants specific details, place names, dates and times—who did what, when and where? The man wants chronology and order. But the boy can't give that to him. The boy has no idea what's coming his way. It's the man who must adjust, who must turn backwards in the search for a meaning.

And so I've come to the comfort of my study to sit and reflect and try to put this down on paper, writing a little each afternoon, for I'm strongest in the afternoons and can handle my pen with some endurance. Luckily my mother isn't around to read this. It probably would have terrified her, and that's not what I want, because I'm not trying to scare anyone. I just want to tell the story to myself, because it is my story. I believe that.

No matter what else may have happened.

I became the man I am today on a humid summer night back in 1961. I still remember the girl, and the kiss, and of course the snakes. If I close my eyes I can still see the sky full of stars. I can hear the crickets droning in the night. I've been looking back on those events in my mind ever since, trying to understand what happened to me then. But the truth of it, the real truth, had always managed to elude me, slipped through my fingers like hot desert sand.

So now I'm letting go of the old man that I've become and I'm drifting back to that rambling country road cutting through the East Texas piney woods. It's August, 1961, and I'm descending from a hot summer sky filled with puffy, gray-bellied clouds, closing in on a white-topped '59 Cadillac as it speeds towards a small, black pocket lake in the distance.

I drift into the car and into the mind of my younger self, who's watching out the window as the landscape rolls by. The air is full of butterflies. They are dying on our windshield with little pops that sound like muffled coughs. I try to turn the bored fifteen-year-old boy's head towards the front seat, where my mother and father are young again, wrapped in the sepia haze of memory, and I listen to the words of the man behind the wheel.

He's pointing off to the right.

"There," he says. "See that?"

The bored fifteen-year-old turns his head. The vegetation, intensely green, thins just enough to reveal the black, moldy shapes of ruined wooden roofs. An abandoned village, many decades old, swallowed up in underbrush.

The boy mutters something, feigning interest.

"That place is called Gaitlinville."

The boy manages a grunt. The fact that his last name, stuck to the suffix —ville seems to mean nothing to him. Undaunted, the father says, "The way my daddy explained it to me, your great-great-grandfather built that village with his brother. Did you know that?"

"You told me that last year," the boy says.

"Oh," my father answers. He catches my eye in the

rearview mirror again and beams a smile. "Did I tell you it's been abandoned since 1904? There's hardly anything left of it these days, but over in Livingston they still tell stories about the weird things that used to go on there."

The boy knows this is an invitation, and he knows what's expected. "Gosh, Dad, what kind of weird things?"

"They were snake handlers, Mark. You know what those are?"

I'm inside the boy's mind completely now. I can see my father's face in the rearview mirror, smiling at me.

I shake my head.

"They're those crazy people who think that God gives them the power to handle poisonous snakes. They don't allow drinking or smoking, but they'll dance around church all day with a fistful of rattlesnakes." He shakes his head and laughs. "Sounds pretty crazy, huh? That's why I hear your great-great-grandfather left. There was supposed to be some kind of feud between him and his brother over that. Doesn't make much sense to me, though. Seems like if the Good Book tells you that you can drink poison and handle snakes without it hurting you it shouldn't be that big of a deal to drink and smoke, you know what I mean?"

Mom gives him a slap on the shoulder. "Joseph, don't be profane."

Good old Mom. We'd never been to church a single day I can remember, but she always did her best to be the Gaitlin family's moral compass.

Dad gooses her thigh, and then gives me a wink in

the rearview mirror.

The boy smiles back obligatorily, but the man inside the boy turns and watches the ruins of the village falling away behind us.

Funny, he thinks, that something so much a part of the past could be so important to the future.

Chapter Two

I was fifteen years old. My hormones were raging out of control. Driving me nuts. My parents were driving me nuts. I was thinking about sex all the time. I thought it would kill me if I didn't get to do it. And, even worse, what if I did do it, and did it wrong. I wanted to be Cary Grant, but when I looked in the mirror all I saw was Bobo the Clown.

Long story short: ninth grade was my own private hell.

And this was supposed to be my summer reprieve.

So, we settled into the cottage where we would be staying for the next two weeks, unpacked, cleaned up, and headed off for the opening night's festivities.

The party was unbearable.

At one point, my mother approached me, a whiskey highball in one hand and a cigarette dangling from the other, and said, "Sweetheart, you're not having a good time, are you?"

I was sitting on a wooden chair by myself, near the backdoor where I had hoped to blend into the wall, my head in my hands.

I looked up at her and blinked.

She raised her eyebrows at me, waiting. I think she was a little drunk.

"I'm sorry, Mom. I…I didn't…what?"

"I said it doesn't look like you're having a very good time."

I tried to smile, but my self-esteem had just been dragged through the mud, and I looked up at her with one of those expressions of indignation and frustration that seems to be the greatest weapon the American teenager can wield against a parent's benevolent cruelty. She had insisted that I wear my white slacks, my white cotton shirt, a skinny black tie, and a powder blue sweater that she swore made me look as handsome as Cary Grant, but that I was convinced made me look more like an organ grinder's monkey. Of course, I almost wished I had the organ grinder's music. That would have at least given the moment a sense of fully realized irony, and it certainly would have been better than The Tuxedo Boys, the band on stage that night. They were up there murdering Sam Cooke's "Everybody Loves to Cha Cha Cha," and they sounded about as natural doing that as I felt in my monkey suit. And then, as my mother and I were having our sitcom moment, The Tuxedo Boys started in on another Sam Cooke tune—this time "Having a Party"—and my mortification was complete. The evening had truly sunk as low as it was going to get.

We were in the Lake Livingston Resort Clubhouse with about two hundred of our closest friends—business associates of my father, mostly—celebrating the arrival of the Great Southern White butterfly in a weeklong festival called The Great White Flight. Sixty years later, as I remember the brigade of white-suited black men standing patiently to serve the guests along the clubhouse walls, drink trays expertly balanced on their fingertips, I can't help but balk at my ignorant complicity in something with so many blatantly racist overtones.

But this was the South in 1961, remember, and I was fifteen and white and wealthy. The first smoke of social revolution had yet to reach my rarified place in the stratosphere.

At the time, all I saw was a room big enough to house a basketball court—the ceiling strung with hand cut lace paper butterflies. This was a yearly event for us, and also for the luminaries of Houston's business community, which back then meant oil. Nearly everyone in the place was in some way or another drawing their lifeblood from an oil pump. My older sister, Jennifer, who was taller and blonder than me, was out on the dance floor, doing the Twist. She thrived here. She was seventeen, dressed in a lettuce green gingham dress, and surrounded by the lean, hungry, clean-shaven faces of a pack of college-aged guys who were looking at her like they were a pride of tweed-coated lions and she was the little fawn they'd just found wandering the veldt.

My mother, undoubtedly, had just witnessed my catastrophically lame attempt to chat up a group of three giggling girls in pink, who all night long had been drifting from one cluster of college boys to the next like a trio of soap bubbles set in motion by a well-scrubbed rendering of the Everly Brothers. Like their song, I was dreaming I was elsewhere, for in reality I was living a nightmare. As soon as I opened my mouth, those girls stopped talking and looked at me, and what they saw was not only a dorky-looking guy dressed as an organ grinder's monkey, but a dorky-looking kid dressed as an organ grinder's monkey. There was an uncomfortable moment of shocked silence accompanied by one of those you've-got-to-be-kidding looks. And then they began to giggle. I walked away from that little nightmare feeling like somebody had just rubbed a dog turd on my face.

So I cleared my throat and said, "No, Mom, not really. I'm not really having that good a time."

Her eyes were red-rimmed and glassy, but compassionate. "I'm sorry, pumpkin."

Somewhere beyond the circle of mother and son the band played on.

Her compassionate frown turned into a sad, sweet

smile, one that was meant to be kind and reassuring, but only managed to make me feel worse.

I buried my hands back into my face.

Then she suddenly brightened. "Hey, pumpkin,"—because she always called me pumpkin when she wanted to cheer me up—"it's only the first night. I bet there'll be plenty more kids your age coming later in the week."

I removed my hands again. "Yeah," I said, trying to force a smile. "Sure."

There was a haze of cigarette smoke near the ceiling. I caught a glimpse of my Dad on the opposite side of the clubhouse. He was laughing and smoking and talking business with some of the other dads.

"Mom?" I said, and gave my voice that polite, hopeful, questioning tone children reserve for when they ask special favors of their parents.

"Yeah, pumpkin?"

"I don't have to stay here, do I? I mean here, in the clubhouse?"

"You're bored, aren't you?"

"Well…" I looked up at her with eyes full of equal parts hope and doubt. "Yeah."

She frowned, like she was thinking about all the reasons why a fifteen-year-old boy shouldn't be allowed to run loose in a strange place after dark. But she was always such a terrible actress when it came to stuff like that, and I knew what her answer was going to be before she said it.

"You know, maybe your sister could introduce you

to…" My mom was a product of her generation, always the moderator, but I have to give her credit where credit is due. She took one look at my face and derailed that train of thought well south of the station.

And that look gave me my chance to escape. The door for freedom was suddenly opening, and I wouldn't have to listen to the lame band anymore. I wouldn't have to be snubbed by pretty girls again. I could escape into the wide-open night.

"Hey, Mom, can I leave my sweater here with you?"

She looked suddenly hurt. "But you look so handsome in that."

"Mom," I said, giving my voice that knowing inflection that suggested we were sharing a secret. Yes, even then, I knew that moms love the idea they are sharing secrets with their kids.

She smiled, a gesture that spoke eloquently of largesse.

"Thanks, Mom."

"Here," she said, "Give it here. Don't stay out too late, okay? I don't mind, but your father wouldn't approve."

To which I fired back with another nonverbal volley—a tragedian's rolling of my eyes.

"I'm serious, buster."

"Yes, ma'am," I said. And you didn't have to tell me twice. I was out of there as fast as the French Army running to the German lines to surrender.

Finally—the sweet taste of freedom. I could feel it in the night air as I walked out the clubhouse doors. Suddenly I could breathe again. The cigarette smoke had filled my lungs, roiling down into the pits of my stomach, where it coiled like a snake.

But suddenly all that was gone.

The scent that took its place was the much cleaner and fresher smell of pine. Back then, you could stand on the shore of Lake Livingston and sweep your eyes across a landscape of skyscraper-sized pine trees stretching off in every direction. In my memory I still see pinecones the size of footballs, dew on the grass like diamonds in the moonlight. In a moment, my parents' world had been replaced by one completely my own. There were no more Tuxedo Boys. No more judgments disguised as giggling girls. There were only the cicadas, droning on and on and on in the night singing their sad insect songs for the world to hear.

So I walked down the trail, towards the boat slips on the eastern tip of the lake—away from the clubhouse—and the farther I got from the noise of my parents' friends and the giggling and that horrible band— they had moved on to Pat Boone's "A Wonderful Time Up There" by that point—the better I felt.

I was one with the night.

The lake water looked black, oily, with puddles of moonlight on the surface. There were butterflies everywhere—the Great Southern Whites in all the trees, fluttering across the red dirt path that led down to the lake. Drunk on the moment, I had a boy's vision of military glory, borrowed from the stories I'd read in the pulps of Sergeant York and Audie Murphy. The butterflies became confetti, and I was a hero riding next to Eisenhower in the back of a black convertible limousine in the midst of a ticker tape parade, the air swarming with the adulation of giggling girls.

Looking around, I could see the darkness that was the piney forest on the opposite side of the lake, a large, black slice of the lake itself, and off to my left, the rows of Queen Anne-style cottages painted in Easter egg colors and topped with peaked gables that were the guests' quarters.

I was following a footpath, browning pine needles neatly and invisibly swept by the help into curb-like piles on either side of me.

My gaze rose from the footpath to the line of trees on the opposite side of the lake, following the shadowed pockets of the forest that rose to the sky, and finally settled on the moldering black lines of Gaitlinville.

I stared at it, fascinated, my mind filled with confused, warring emotions. The buildings were barely visible in the darkness and dense underbrush. All I could really see of the place that bore my name was a black corner of a sagging roof and a leaning, windowless wall. But the rest of the village was there, back there somewhere in all that underbrush, and for the moment, it held me in sway.

I knew the story of its founding well enough. My dad's descriptions in the car were hardly necessary. My great-great grandfather, Abraham Gaitlin, and his brother,

Ulysses Gaitlin, had founded the little town in 1838. They were awarded the three hundred acre plot of forestland by Stephen F. Austin's Austin Colony as recompense for their service in the Texas War for Independence from Mexico. Abraham, my great-great grandfather, was the practical one of the pair, the farmer, the planner, and the administrator. But his brother Ulysses was the spiritual one, and so he was the natural leader. I had read one of his early sermons once, a horribly obtuse and rambling tract of the John Winthrop "City upon a Hill" variety, yet filled with more doom and gloom than anything the Massachusetts Bay Colony ever had to endure. After reading that, it was little wonder to me that my great-great-grandfather would make the split that divorced our family from a claim to this land. Grandpa told me Abraham made it eleven years before he left, but I know it wouldn't have taken me that long.

And then I heard a noise.

Splashing water.

Someone was swimming in the water.

I turned from the village in the trees and listened.

The swimmer made no sounds beyond the splashing that one usually makes when lazily swimming in a lake at night. I heard arms cutting into the water, feet kicking slowly, but nothing more. No sounds of distress.

Thoughts of family feuds faded. I wondered who could be swimming out here. Everyone else was supposed to be back at the clubhouse listening to the band.

Well—almost everyone—except for this mysterious swimmer and me.

I had every intention of being quiet, but I had to see who was swimming. I peeked through the pine branches to see what I could see.

The pier jutted out into the water like a big capital letter T dropped on its back, moonlight dappling on the tops of the small, glassy ripples.

And floating on the water, on her back, her fingers tinkling on the surface of the water like it was a piano keyboard, was a very beautiful—and very naked—girl my age.

I swallowed hard, and nearly had to push down the lump that had formed in my throat. I glanced back in the direction from which I had come and saw the clubhouse at the top of the hill. Chinese paper lanterns on strings encircled the yard in front of the clubhouse, and a buttery glow of yellow light leaked out onto the grass from the open front door. The sounds of the party were faint and far away. I looked at my watch and saw it was only half past eight; the party still had another three hours to go at least before the guests started wandering back to their cottages. There was time for this.

I turned back to the water and watched the girl. She had long dark hair and wasn't wearing a stitch of clothing. Naked for the world to see.

Now, like most boys, I had had the misfortune of accidentally walking in on my mom and my older sister naked. You open the bathroom door, and there, screaming at you to close the damn door, is the nightmare of your own flesh and blood, naked. At that moment, they're not girls, or even ladies. They're your mom, or your sister. They're blood. And that is eye opening. It's gross. It's embarrassing. Kind of disgusting, really.

But this, this was not my mom. And this was not my sister. This was a sixteen-year-old girl, with small, perfect breasts and a flat tummy and a curvaceous bottom and a long ribbon of dark hair that curled around her shoulders as she turned and turned again in the water. And when my eyes fell on her it was like standing on the edge of a very high cliff and looking down: my legs suddenly felt weak and my stomach turned in knots. I couldn't have looked away, not for all the tea in China.

Entranced, scarcely knowing what I was doing, I left my little hiding spot and stumbled down the dirt trail and out to the tip of the pier.

She heard me, and let out a startled sound.

Her body dropped into the water, so that only her head and shoulders and hands were visible.

She looked at me then, not reproachfully, as I no doubt deserved, but simply looked at me as she effortlessly treaded water.

For a moment I thought there was something vaguely alien about her features—but then I wasn't sure. And the longer I looked, the less sure I became. Her skin tone was as white bread as mine, but there was something about her features that I couldn't place. Her perfectly round eyes maybe or her wide, thin lips that made her mouth look not quite right. But fifteen-year-old boys are not art critics, and when there's a naked girl in front of them, they tend to see only the stunning wonder that God intended in such delights, focusing on the good stuff. She was naked, and that was about all my hormone-doped mind was capable of registering. There are very few deal breakers at that point.

"I didn't mean to startle you," I said.

We looked at each other, and for the first time in a long time, the noise of The Tuxedo Boys filled the night again.

"So, going for a swim, huh?"

As soon as I said it I winced and nearly kicked myself.

Smooth as Cary Grant I am not.

She smiled, then kicked her legs and came up so that she was floating on her back again. My eyes went straight to her breasts and my mouth filled with saliva and my slacks became suddenly tight. I swallowed hard—then snatched a quick glance back at the clubhouse. No change there.

"My name's Mark Gaitlin. Are you, uh, staying a-round here?"

She rolled over in the water and smiled. Then she pointed vaguely towards the piney woods on the opposite shore.

Towards Gaitlinville.

"You're staying over there?" I said. I was momen-tarily confused, but then my hormones swept all that away. It didn't really matter. What really mattered was that I was a fifteen-year-old boy talking to a girl who was skinny dipping in a lake.

The equation doesn't get simpler than that.

She turned, swam a little closer, then hooked one finger up in the air and used it to gesture me into the water.

"Uh," I said, and pointed at my chest.

She nodded.

"Me?"

She nodded again. This was like talking to a mute person.

"You want me to come swimming…with you?"

Her smile widened and she nodded again.

"Can't you talk?" I said, and then wished I hadn't said it.

I was stalling.

I tried to come up with something clever to say, to prove I was a fifteen-year-old Cary Grant, but all I could manage was to mutter, "Um, okay, well—when in Rome."

I knelt down and untied my shoestrings. My hands were shaking so badly I could barely close my fingers around the laces. But I managed. I tossed my shoes off onto the dock behind me. I untied my thin black tie and discarded my shirt and eventually even my white slacks. I got everything off but my boxers and then just stood there, looking at her looking back up at me. I swallowed and you could hear the booming of my heart over the sickening sounds of a Bob Wills & The Texas Playboys cover.

I was about as nervous as I could be, and yeah, I was embarrassed about getting naked in front of a girl. I was fifteen, for Christ's sake.

So what I did was I took a step or two towards the edge of the pier, like I was going to jump in just as I was, my terrified manly parts still tucked safe and sound inside my boxers.

And then I looked down.

She was looking up at me, her lower lip pushed out in a pout that made me feel like a jackass. I tried to speak and couldn't. I put my thumbs inside the waistband of my boxers and said, "You want me to…" and couldn't get the rest out.

She smiled again. Nodded.

I gulped.

"Okay," I said.

Now stop me if you've heard this one before. There were these two bulls standing on the top of a hill, looking down at a herd of cows in the pasture below. The young bull turns to the old bull and says, "Hey, I bet if we run on down there we can catch one of them cows and screw it." The older bull just shakes his head and says, "I got a better idea. Let's walk down there and screw all of them."

Ba dum bum.

Thank you folks, I'm here all week. Don't forget to tip your bar and wait staff. Is this thing on?

But seriously, the moral of that joke, at least as near

as I can tell, is that with age comes wisdom. Now I don't want to pretend for a moment that I had anything remotely close to wisdom at that age. The young bull in that joke, that was me all the way. I was rushing headlong towards that great golden moment when I could throw my virginity out the window and cruise that miracle mile of magical loving any time I wanted. My friends and I back in school talked about it constantly. We talked about when it was going to happen, who had already done it, which girls we might be able to talk into doing it with us. But when it came right down to it…well, if I'd been wearing boots, I would have been shaking in them.

So I closed my eyes and down came my boxer shorts.

I braced for her giggle.

None came.

I opened my eyes, and there she was, smiling at me.

Then she turned and swam away from the pier.

I traced the line of her spine down her back and saw the curve of her buttocks break the surface of the water. They were silvered by moonlight.

"All right," I said, sensing that I had just crossed some kind of personal Rubicon. I jumped in.

We swam together for a few minutes without talking—or, more precisely, without her talking. I made a few clumsy remarks about how good the water felt, about how nice a night it was. You come here often? But she merely smiled and swam around and turned and turned in the water, seemingly without the slightest modesty in showing me her bare body.

And what a nice body it was.

I asked her name, and she turned away and swam around some more. She had a languid, easy stroke. I could tell she was a gifted swimmer, for I was no slouch myself, and I couldn't match her sudden bursts of careless speed. She didn't even look like she was trying. She would turn and speed off and then rejoin her elliptical orbit back toward the pier, where I was. She barely made a splash.

By the time she returned to me I was done talking and decided to just let whatever was going to happen happen. I swam, and enjoyed her smile when she flashed it my way, and thrilled at the sight of her bare breasts and buttocks whenever those made an appearance. Galahad basking in the glow of the Grail. That was me looking at those lovely breasts in the moonlight. They were exquisite.

It occurred to me then that not one of the guys I knew back in school was going to believe that this little encounter had actually happened, and I was wondering what I could do to garner some proof when the girl suddenly ducked under the water. She hadn't done that yet, gone all the way under, and it surprised me. I looked around for where she would surface.

Then she was in front of me, her nipples grazing along the skin of my chest, our lips so close we were practically kissing. I could feel the heat of her breath on my lips, her body against mine.

"Hi," I said nervously. "I never caught your name?"

"Ermelinde," she said softly. Her voice was just as lovely as the rest of her.

"That's a pretty name..." was all I was able to get out. The tip of her tongue appeared between her lips and lingered there, and then she reached forward and put her lips on mine, and we were kissing. I felt clumsy, but also wonderful. Her tongue pushed into my mouth. My heart was pumping so fast I thought I was going to die.

Getting back to the young and old bulls.

I used to be the young bull. I've since become the old bull. My wife—Suzanne and I have been married for forty-three years now—may disagree with me on this, but I think I've learned a thing or two about subtlety in the bedroom over the years. I've learned you get the best results when you ease a woman into sex. You need heat and passion and spontaneity, certainly, and creativity, and a certain amount of chemistry—but what it boils to is that a woman is like a race car: you need to heat up the tires a little if you want to get the best traction.

But, like I said, back then, when I had Ermelinde in my arms, I was the young bull. I was about that subtle when I reached up and put a hand on each of her breasts. They were cold and wet and firm and felt wonderful in my hands.

She backed away from me instantly. I felt like she had just cut the electrical current running between us. My body was still pumping out that electricity, but now it had no place to go.

"What?" I said.

She just stared at me.

"I'm sorry," I apologized.

She smiled, but it was a different smile than the one she had given me earlier. There was no encouragement in it: it was more of a sad smile, a farewell smile.

She turned and swam away.

"Hey," I said. "Please don't leave. What did I do wrong? I won't touch you again. Where are you going?"

She climbed the ladder to the pier and took down an ochre-colored cotton dress that was hanging from a nail on one of the beams.

She slipped it over her head and straightened it.

"Wait," I said. There was a pathetic whine in my voice that I couldn't control. "Please don't leave. I'm sorry. I promise I won't do that again."

But she was already walking back up the pier towards the shore.

I swam for the ladder and shot up to the deck. She was on the shore then, body bent forward as she climbed the dirt path that led up to the main walking path. There was a wrecked sailboat there, and I lost sight of her as she hooked a right turn around it.

I started down the pier, wet feet slapping on the wooden planks, realized I was still naked, and then turned back to dress as quickly as I could. By the time I got my shoes on, nearly a minute had gone by. I ran for the main path, hoping to catch up with her and apologize—hell, I would have done just about anything to get her naked again, even if it meant not being able to touch her—but she was long gone. She had simply disappeared into the night.

I stood there next to that wrecked sailboat and let my mind race. I couldn't believe it. The greatest experience of my short life had just ended, and I had no idea why.

Well, I understood why. I just didn't understand why what I had done had made her so mad.

I sighed.

And then, out of the corner of my eye, I saw movement.

I looked down at the little crevice beneath the wrecked hull and saw a copperhead slowly unfolding from its hiding place in the shadows. It was a big one, four feet long, with a thick, round body that glistened in the moonlight. Its banded hues of pine needle brown and rust red and coppery yellow were deceptively beautiful. I couldn't help but stare.

I remembered something I'd once read about copperheads in a Max Brand western, that their camouflage is so perfect you can often times be looking right at one and never even know it. In fact, they don't strike the way a rattlesnake does. Instead, they simply bite, and most of the people who get bit by them do so because they accidentally step or sit on them.

I shook myself loose from the haze I was in just as the snake had crossed most of the distance between us and I hurriedly jogged back up to the main path.

The copperhead continued towards me for a few feet, but then turned away and slithered off into the undergrowth at the tree line.

It wasn't until after that I realized I had been holding my breath.

Chapter Three

I still made it home before my parents and my sister. I took a hot shower, dried off, and then crawled into bed. I felt mentally exhausted, though my body was still humming like a live wire.

I tried to sleep, but I tossed fitfully, and every time I closed my eyes I saw Ermelinde's naked body gliding through the water. I imagined what it would be like to see her again and if she'd forgive me for trying to feel her up and if she'd let me touch more of her next time.

Eventually I drifted into sleep, and yet I don't think I ever went completely under. Instead, I lingered at the edge of sleep, aware I was dreaming and yet unable to stop the dream from coming.

I dreamt I was wandering through the woods at night and came upon a little village of some thirty or so buildings, most of them unpainted and weathered and possessing an unmistakable lean-to quality, but still remarkably preserved. Night turned to day unnoticed in the dream's easy, slipstream logic. The spongy, damp ground beneath my feet became a dirt road through the middle of the village, hazy with dust and golden lances of light.

This was Gaitlinville and it was completely abandoned. I could feel its stillness like a curtain, and yet it wasn't a totally unpleasant feeling being in the midst of that desolation. I felt instead an easy familiarity with the austere, pioneer architecture; almost as if I could say the names of the families that once lived in the homes I passed, if only I could focus hard enough.

I walked on steadily. I saw three larger buildings off to my left and the spire of a church to my right, a small, moldy graveyard beyond that. The graves were covered with a blanket of brown pine needles. As I walked towards the church, drawn by the stillness of the air around me, I happened to glance into one of the open doorways to my left and saw that shelves of the store were still laden with goods. A thick grime of dust covered everything, and curtains of cobwebs hung from the shelves. I was intrigued by the sight of all those unused goods and I turned that way, when suddenly I heard voices from up ahead.

I wasn't frightened. I turned toward the church and saw shadowy figures moving inside the open front door. The voices seemed to move together then, becoming patterns, forming the textured rhythm of a fearfully eager chanting.

I moved closer.

Standing at the doorway it took a moment for my eyes to adjust to the gloom. Inside, I saw a group of men and women gathered around an old, gray-haired hag on her back on the altar. Her knees were up in the air and spread far apart, her simple brown dress gathered around her hips. She was moaning in pain, her face awash with sweat, the hair matted to her forehead. Her eyes had a fevered shine and they rolled wildly from side to side while her mouth twisted into a grimace. My first thought was that she was giving birth, but as the others chanted and cavorted about her, I could see that wasn't the case. Her lower body was changing, writhing, sloughing off her human form as the banded, flopping mass of a snake's tail emerged. The tail flailed at the air and then the woman's whole body twisted round, slapping the wooden floor with a great undulating roll of reptilian muscle. She was on her stomach now, holding her torso off the floor with her hands. She turned toward me for the first time then, the slits of her perfectly round yellow eyes locking on mine, and I staggered back into the sunlight, the back of my hand jammed into my mouth to hold down the scream.

"My God," I muttered.

"Your God isn't here," said Ermelinde.

I turned toward her, but she was already walking away, behind the church. In the fluid logic of the dream it seemed perfectly normal, and I followed her.

We passed through the graveyard and the sunlight seemed to shrink away from the headstones. Ermelinde crossed the field of headstones. At the other side was a dark pond covered in green algae. She undid her dress and let it fall to her feet. And the next instant, she was stepping into the pond.

I looked down and saw I was naked too. I stepped into the pool and swarm toward her. She moved in close and I put my hands on her breasts and they felt even better, softer than they had before, as if they were made to fit my hands. She moaned softly, her body moving in time with mine, writhing with pleasure as the wind moved the trees and filled the air with the odor of pine.

This time, I put my hands on the curve of her bottom and pulled her closer.

She parted her lips and her tongue slid into my mouth.

Then her tongue swelled and swelled like a moving snake inside my mouth, pushing itself deeper down my throat until it was choking me, and I woke up screaming.

Chapter Four

The next morning, I had breakfast with my family at the restaurant on the second floor of the clubhouse. Afterwards, my dad drank coffee and read the *Houston Chronicle* while my sister chattered my mom's ear off about the boy she'd met the night before.

"He goes to Yale, Momma, and he's Phi Beta Kappa," Jennifer said. "His name is Cole Prescott."

"A college boy," Mom said, and I could tell she was wincing inside. Like I said, my mom was never much of an actress when it came to disguising her concern, and I could tell she was choking on her urge to squash the flame of passion before it had a chance to spread up under my sister's dress.

"I know his father," my dad said. "Will Prescott. Does corporate real estate law. Good man." He folded his paper down and gave me a pat on the shoulder. "He's a partner in Senator Howelton's firm. Might be a good contact for you to make."

"Dear," my mom said to my dad. "He's fifteen. Fifteen-year-old boys don't make contacts."

Good ole Mom, reading my face like a book.

Dad waved her objection away. "I'm just saying it's not too early to start thinking about this kind of stuff." To me he said, "You're gonna need a senator's endorsement to get into West Point."

He smiled all around the table. Old story, his desire to see me tossing my white hat into the air at my graduation from West Point.

Then the smile wavered and he said, "You still want to go to West Point, don't you?"

I stammered out something about not being sure what college I wanted to go to, but evidently it lacked enough conviction for him.

He said, "I thought you still wanted to go to West Point," and waited.

"Dear," Mom said, "maybe he's changed his mind."

"What do you mean he's changed his mind?" To me, he said, "When did you change your mind?"

"I don't really want to go to West Point, Dad…" I said, and sort of trailed off into a murmur.

"If you don't want to go there, son, that's fine." He

took a deep, disappointed breath. He said, "Look, I just want you to be interested in something. The world isn't going to wait for you to make up your mind, you know. If you take too long, it'll run you over like a locomotive in the middle of the night."

My mom, God love her, put her slender fingers on the back of my dad's hand and said, "Let me warm up your coffee, dear."

He turned to her. "Huh? Oh, okay. Thanks."

Mom topped off his coffee cup and spooned in a little sugar.

My dad leaned back in his chair, and for a moment I thought he was going to try to restart the conversation.

Thank God he didn't.

Mom had successfully broken his momentum. She could always do that.

Dad had just turned forty-five that July, and he looked strong, healthy, and upwardly mobile. He had a slender build, an athlete's body that still looked like an athlete's body inside his powder blue short-sleeve shirt and gray slacks. Back then, he wore Brylcreem in his hair and always had it slicked back from his forehead, and looking at pictures of him from those days, I could tell he must have been considered a good looking man. His face was angular, strong, sophisticated. His eyes were spaced wide apart, and stared back at you with the calm self-assurance of a man who knows his own worth. Some men, when you look into their eyes, you just know they were destined to reach the top of the game, and that was my dad. Never any doubt about where he was going or what he needed to do to get there.

But me? Well, I was no Cary Grant with the ladies, and I wasn't the political animal my father was, either. Going to West Point had never really been my idea. The year before, my dad told me about one of his friends who had just been named a federal judge. He told me the man's life story, how he had gone to West Point, and then served in the JAG before entering civilian law as a federal prosecutor. My dad walked away from that conversation having convinced himself that I wanted to go to West Point and be an Army officer. I walked away feeling numb.

So, while my mom stroked the back of his hand, and my sister prattled on about boys, I turned my attention toward the lake. The restaurant was open-air, basically a giant balcony that jutted over the water like the prow of a battleship. I watched as hundreds of thousands of white butterflies fluttered over the perfectly green lawns and through the trees, everything touched by an early morning haze of golden sunlight. It was beautiful, pristine in a way you just don't see anymore, and my mind turned back to the night before. I looked down at the pier and thought of the naked girl in the water.

Yeah, Dad, I said with an inward laugh, I'm interested in something all right. But you are never gonna guess what.

Chapter Five

After breakfast, we split up and went our separate ways.

As I was going downstairs, I ran into a kid I'd met the year before named Randy Worley. His dad was an attorney, like mine—every kid out here had an attorney for a dad, it seemed—but his dad did mineral rights law for the independent wildcatters, which was an uneven way of making a living to say the least. To borrow a phrase from my dad, it was feast or famine for *those people*—the negative emphasis always on *those people* when he talked about wildcatters.

Notice I didn't say Randy was a friend—because

he wasn't.

And, no, it wasn't because of anything my dad said about wildcatters.

I had my own very good reasons for thinking little of Randy Worley. In fact, though I'd only hung out with him for less than a week the year before, by the end of that week, I was lying awake at night thinking of ways to kill him and make it look like an accident.

You see, the resort did all these activities for the kids each year. There was a two-man tug-o-war and an egg toss and potato sack races and all the other stupid things adults can think of to keep kids busy. You know what they say about idle hands.

Well, the year before, Randy and I had been almost exactly the same size. We were both leaning just a little to the athletic side of average, both reasonably good at sports in a my-dad-is-making-me-do-this kind of way, and so it was natural that we got teamed up against each other in all the little activities that populated the days of bored fourteen-year-olds on vacation with their parents.

The thing about Randy was that he was annoyingly competitive. I remember, right before the tug-o-war, he stood there telling me how all he wanted to do was get out of there, how all the stupid events they organized for us were just lame kid stuff.

"Wouldn't it be cool if we both just dropped the rope when they said 'Go!' and walked away?" he said. "You know, really show 'em how lame it all is."

"Yeah," I said, "I guess."

And then it was our turn and we went out there. We picked up our respective ends of the rope, and the next thing you know, Randy is across the mud pit from me, every blood vessel in his arms and his neck standing out through his skin like cords as he tried to drag me into the mud. He caught me totally off guard, and of course I went face first into the mud. When I looked up, everybody in the crowd was laughing, and Randy was laughing the hardest of all.

Needless to say, I hated him after that. And needless to say, I was not glad to see him this year.

I did get one small consolation though. While I had grown steadily over the past year, filling out more or less evenly, poor Randy had shot up almost half a foot. He was a lot taller than me now, but he was as gangly looking as they come. And—thank you, Lord—his face had erupted into a minefield of zits, blackheads like mountaintops seen from low orbit.

I smiled inwardly as we shook hands.

"Did you get your license yet?" he asked. Back then, the legal driving age in Texas was fourteen if you qualified for a hardship license, fifteen if you didn't.

"Sure did," I said. "Been driving since February."

"Oh," he said, his mean little smile wavered just enough to notice. "That's cool."

"You?"

"Yeah," he said. "I got mine last month."

First blood, I thought. So far so good.

But then he hit me below the belt. "Have you gone

to see the Oilers play yet?"

My smile faded. The Houston Oilers were charter members of the AFL back in 1960. That was long before the Astrodome was built, of course. They were still playing at Jeppeson Stadium back then, not far from our house in River Oaks; but despite my dad's repeated promises, and despite the fact that they'd been playing in Houston for two full seasons, I had yet to see a game.

"No," I said, and braced myself for what was coming.

"I've been to four games so far," he said, and held up four fingers on his right hand and wriggled them at me, just in case I didn't know how many four was. "And you know who I got to see?"

"Who?" I said.

"I got to see Billy Cannon score four touchdowns in one game. That guy is amazing. You have got to go see him play."

"I think I heard that game on the radio," I said, and tried to sound indifferent. Actually, I remembered hearing it on the radio very well. I remembered every word of it. I remembered you could actually hear the bleachers rumbling in the background.

"Hearing it isn't the same thing as seeing it," he said with a superior air. "That's just lame."

The little worm of meanness and jealousy that had been crawling around inside my guts began to roar. Billy Cannon had won the Heisman when he was playing for Louisiana State, and he went on to guide the Oilers to two straight championships in 1960 and 1961. More than ever before, I wanted to reach out and strangle Randy Worley.

"My dad even got him to sign a football for me."

It's a pity the things you hear when you don't have a gun, I thought.

Dad never did get the time to take me to a game, and of course the Oilers are no more for this world. These days, they're called the Tennessee Titans. And the Astrodome, where they used to play, is closed down and probably due to be torn down, if it hasn't been torn down already. Those grand old days are gone, but the hurt Randy Worley gave me that day is still with me. God, what I would have given to see Billy Cannon play.

But of course I didn't, and Randy Worley did, and he took no end of pleasure in reminding me of the fact.

Finally, just to keep from killing him, I guided the conversation to the one area where I knew we were on even footing—pulp westerns. The two of us were crazy for them, and the fact that Randy knew that George Owen Baxter, Martin Dexter, Evin Evans, David Manning, and Max Brand were all the same person was probably the one thing that saved him from a horrible death at my hands. The year before we had traded several back issues of *Argosy* between us, and I asked him if he'd brought any more with him.

"I'm into somebody new," he said. "You ever heard of J. Frank Dobie?"

"No," I said. "I've been reading a lot of Bret Harte

lately."

"Bret Harte is a homosexual," he said, though he pronounced it 'Homer-sexual.' I got to tell you the truth, though. I didn't notice. To me, with my East Texas accent, 'homer-sexual' sounded like the right way to say it.

He smiled at my lack of recognition. "J. Frank Dobie, man, his stuff is cool. He writes about early Texas history. But not the boring stuff, you know what I mean? He does stories about the Texas Rangers and stuff like that."

"Sounds neat," I said. And yeah, I was genuinely intrigued.

"You bet it is. He has this one story about a Ranger named Jack Webb—you know who that is?"

"Sure," I said. "They named a county for him down near Laredo."

"That's right. Well, Jack Webb is chasing this bad guy through the Chisos Mountains out in West Texas. So he's chasing him, and it's been raining real hard for like the whole week before this, right? There's all these washed out creek beds and stuff in the area. Well, they get in this running gunfight, and Jack shoots the guy's horse by mistake. The guy tries to run away on foot, but ends up slipping into one of those washed out creek beds." Randy paused there for dramatic effect. "You know what he fell into?"

"What?" I said.

"A bolus of rattlesnakes."

I blinked at him. "A what?"

"You never heard about that?"

"No," I said.

Randy Worley puffed himself up and took on the air of the guy who is the first in his circle of friends to lose his virginity.

"A bolus is what snakes do when they're having sex."

That pretty much froze me, left me with nothing to say. I had pictured me having sex, of course, but never snakes.

"They get all knotted together into a ball, you know, like a ball of rubber bands, except they're all moving all the time. Usually it's a bunch of snakes that get together for it. There are stories of people seeing a bolus four feet thick." He paused, savoring the horror on my face, and said, "In the J. Frank Dobie story, he says Jack Webb heard this fella screaming, but when he looked into the spot where the guy fell, he was already dead." He snapped his fingers. "Happened that fast."

We had made it downstairs and out the side door. The Great Southern Whites were everywhere, thick as ball moss on the trees and filling the air like snow.

A black man came out of the door with a garbage can full of cups and streamers and cigarette butts and smiled at us.

"Good morning, gentlemen," he said. "How are you fine sirs doin'?"

Randy ignored him. I nodded. I felt vaguely uncomfortable, a grown man calling me sir, but I didn't know why it bothered me. I do now, of course, but back then, like I've said, I was the young bull.

The black man carried his garbage can over to a waiting truck. He carried a litter stick with a sharp point to pick up trash.

As I watched the man work, my discomfort grew. I knew the resort prided itself on making this part of the business invisible to guests' eyes, and that our witnessing it was more a result of the inclination of young boys to find mischief than carelessness on the part of the management, but it still made me uncomfortable. Like I said, basking in the warm glow of complacency was a perk of the well-to-do back then, and no doubt still is. But I think little moments like that were the seeds of the ugly self-realization that lay ahead for my generation in the next ten years.

Randy said, "Wait for me, okay?"

"Where you goin'? I asked.

"Gonna drain the lizard," he said, and winked obscenely. "Back in a flash."

He sprinted off to the bathroom, leaving me standing there. The old black groundskeeper came back and lifted the trash can up so he could put it into its wooden container. I was only half watching him, because I was still feeling uncomfortable, and when he dropped the metal can it made a crash that caused me to nearly jump out of my shoes.

I looked over at him and saw the pain on his face, his hand holding the small of his lower back like he was trying to keep it from springing out of his skin.

I ran over to him.

"Hey, mister, you okay?"

With his eyes closed he took a couple of deep breaths. Then he opened his eyes and smiled at me.

"Got a back like an old broke dog," he mused. "Yeah, I'm okay."

I nodded.

He lifted the trashcan again, and I could see the hurt on his face. I reached over and helped him lift it into the wooden crate.

"I appreciate that, young sir," he said. "Thank you."

"Yes, sir."

He laughed. "My name's Ben Morris," he said. "You don't have to call me 'sir.' Ben'll do me just fine."

I nodded again. I was feeling really uncomfortable now. He seemed to read my discomfort and the smile went out of his face. All the light and friendliness that had been there was gone and in its place I saw the neutral, blank expression that blacks from that time got so good at showing to the world when they were around whites. All at once there was nothing to like and nothing to get upset with. He was one of the help again, nothing more, nothing less.

He turned away.

Suddenly I felt really, really bad. I had just behaved like an ass and I knew it. He had been friendly to me, but my reaction had shoved that friendliness back in his face. Like I said, the winds of change had yet to reach my rarified position of wealth and privilege, but I was feeling a drop in the barometric pressure.

And the thing was, race had nothing to do with it.

"Sir, I'm sorry," I said to his back.

He turned and looked at me.

"That was rude of me. I'm sorry. My dad says if you call a grown-up by his first name it's a sign of disrespect. I didn't mean to be rude."

He stared at me for a moment longer, and then the smile slowly spread over his features once again.

"What's your name?" he asked.

"Mark Gaitlin," I said.

The smile bled out of his face so fast I thought I had done something else to offend him.

I said, "I'm sorry, did I—"

"You from the same Gaitlins what built that village up yonder?"

There was an unmistakable hostility in his tone and in his stance now that made me feel afraid.

"Sort of," I said. "My great-great-grandfather was Abraham Gaitlin. He founded that village up there, from what they tell me. But he left it a long time ago."

Ben stared at me. He was tall and slender, with a narrow, angular face and small, black eyes. He had a full head of hair that was clouded over with gray, making it look almost piebald. But it was those eyes of his that caused me to back up. They were so intimidating, stern and hard that for a moment I actually thought of running away.

"That's a bad place up there," he said darkly. "A real bad place."

I didn't know what to make of that, so I just stared.

"You said you're of Abraham Gaitlin's line?"

"That's right," I said. I could hear the tremor in my voice and I tried to compensate for it by standing up straight.

"Well, I guess you wouldn't been of Ulysses Gaitlin's line. Ain't been none of them around these parts since 1889. Not since your…your what, great-grandfather?"

"Abraham Gaitlin was my great-great-grandfather," I said.

He nodded thoughtfully. "Not since your great-great-grandfather and his brother had that fallin' out over their mother's grave."

My fear was rapidly giving way to curiosity. In just a few words this stranger had managed to tell me more about my own family than I'd ever heard before.

My hands fell down by my side. In spite of myself I took a step toward him. "What do you mean over their mother's grave? I never heard anything about that."

He looked like he didn't believe me. "You mean to tell me you don't know nothin' about your own family?"

I shook my head.

"My dad told me Abraham Gaitlin left because the rest of the village was a bunch of snake handlers who wouldn't drink or smoke."

Ben laughed derisively. "That's what he told you?"

I nodded.

"And you didn't bother to ask any questions?"

"No," I said.

Now it was Ben's turn to shake his head. The smile returned, but it wasn't warm like it had been. He actually seemed to pity me.

"They was snake handlers all right, but it weren't no Pentecostal revival goin' on up there. Ulysses Gaitlin and his kin were into all kinds of weirdness, snake cults and devil worship and stuff like that. My daddy said there was nights right after Abraham Gaitlin left that you could hear singin' and chantin' goin' on up there through the trees all night long. People had seen strange lights climbing up to the sky."

"I don't believe that," I said. "Randy put you up to telling me some kind of Clark Ashton Smith story."

"I don't know nobody named Smith," Ben said. "But I ain't tellin' you no story neither. That great-great-grandfather of yours, he and his brother had themselves a nasty fallin' out over how they was gonna bury their momma. Ulysses Gaitlin, he wouldn't let Abraham put the woman in the ground. He said he help her sluff off her mortal coil and become something…else. I don't know what. But it was right after that that your great-great-grandfather come down through the trees and walked into Livingston and got drunk for four days straight. Nobody knows what happened to him after that."

"He was a lawyer in Houston," I said.

"Hmm," Ben said, chewing on his bottom lip.

I was confused, and angry too. Though I was receptive to the idea of social change that was brewing in the air, I was still a child of wealth, and an inculcated sense of white entitlement was part of my upbringing—and here a black man had just called my family a bunch of devil worshipping weirdos. I keep feeling like I ought to apologize for the way I was brought up, but at that moment, I felt like I had every right to be offended at his impertinence.

The air between us felt charged. I could feel my face heating up from my anger and I felt like I had to say something to rise to my family's defense.

But I didn't get the chance.

He nodded to himself, as though he had just made up his mind about something, and said, "Listen, you do yourself a favor, you hear? Don't be goin' up around that village. It's a bad place. A real bad place."

"I'll keep it in mind," I said.

He nodded again and turned and walked off.

I watched him go, my anger mellowing into an insolated blanket of smug superiority.

Randy appeared at my side.

"You all right?"

"Yeah," I said. I wanted to put the unpleasantness out of my head, so I said, "I saw a snake last night."

"You did? What kind?"

"Copperhead."

"No way," Randy said. "You sure?"

"Sure I'm sure."

"Where?"

"Down by the pier." I pointed to where I'd seen the naked girl. I had no intention of telling Randy Worley about her, but I thought it might be a chance to see if she was there.

"Let's go," he said.

So we walked down the red dirt path that led to the pier and he talked about J. Frank Dobie and the adventures of the Texas Rangers and I thought about what I would say to my lady friend if—no, check that, I told myself—when I saw her again.

But when we got to the pier she wasn't there. I don't know why I expected her to be there, but I did. A boy's vanity, I guess. Stand still and watch the world go round about me.

"Where'd you see it?" he asked.

I showed him the old wrecked sailboat and we poked around the pine needles with sticks, but of course the snake wasn't there, either.

"Could be anywhere in all these pine needles," he said.

Then he stopped, looked around, and took out a pack of Pall Malls. He offered me one.

"Are you kidding?" I said. "My mom would chop my balls off if she caught me smoking."

"Yeah, like you're gonna be using 'em anyway."

I snatched the cigarette out of his hand. "Thanks," I said. I took a drag and started coughing for dear life.

"Feels good, huh?" he asked.

I looked at him and hated him. "I smoke all the

time," I said, as I started another coughing fit. My throat felt raw, my lungs felt like they were on fire, but I kept smoking anyway.

He raised one eyebrow at me in a superior, smug bastard kind of way. Some people, you can hate. But for some, there's this special degree of hatred. And Randy had long before promoted himself to the ninth level of my hell.

Chapter Six

"Dad," I said, "what's a bolus?"

We were at lunch in the clubhouse—pork chops with mashed potatoes and black-eyed peas. I was sitting between my dad and my sister, on the opposite side of the table and downwind from my mom, just to minimize the chances of her figuring out what I'd been up to. My sister kept leaning towards me and sniffing, though, and I finally had to kick her in the leg to get her to cut it out.

My dad gave me a strange look, looked into my eyes trying to find why in the world I'd asked him such a strange question, then finally said, "A bolus is any kind of round, soft mass. It can also refer to a round pill veterinarians give to horses."

"Oh. Okay." Dad is a walking dictionary.

He added, "Where in the world did you hear that word?"

"A guy I know," I said, noncommittally.

My mom said, "Did you meet a friend, pumpkin?"

Jennifer leaned close to me and sniffed me. I kicked her again, which did nothing but make her giggle.

"What's this boy's name?" my dad said. "Do I know him?"

"Maybe," I said.

"What's his name?"

I looked down at my half-eaten pork chop. "Randy Worley," I said.

"Worley?" my dad echoed. "His dad's Peter Worley, the mineral rights guy."

"Um, I'm not sure."

"He is," my dad said. He let out a grunt that summed up his feelings for Peter Worley with perfect clarity. He turned to my mom and said, "He does mineral rights law for independent wildcatters."

"Oh," my mom said.

"What were you guys doing?" my sister said, and gave me a look that said I was only seconds away from disaster at her hands.

"Are you two going to be running around together this week?" my dad asked cautiously.

"No," I said.

Dad brightened a little. "He's that boy you had the

tug-o'war match with last year, right?"

"Yes, sir."

"I remember that," my sister said. "He pulled you right into the mud. I seem to remember there were a bunch of girls watching, too. Hey, Mark, I bet most of those girls'll be back this year."

"Jenny," my mom said, "please."

"Well, maybe this year you'll give it back to him, eh?" Dad reached over and gave me a that's-my-boy punch in the shoulder.

"Yes, sir," I said.

Dad ordered a refill of his iced tea from the waiter and then said, "So why'd you want to know what a bolus is, Mark?"

My mom and sister were both looking at me now. Mom had that sweet, but still sort of sad smile on her face that indicated, in her eyes at least, I was still her little baby. Jenny's smile was just wicked.

I cleared my throat.

These days, both my wife and I are retired, but when she was working, my wife taught Victorian Literature at the University of Texas in Austin. Now I don't know if you know what English faculties are like, but you get a pretty eclectic mix of conservatives and left wing liberals and hard core feminists and even a few new age weirdos. About the only thing they all have in common is a love of reading and a love of drinking, and when they get together at parties, well, they usually get pretty drunk.

So I was drunk at one of those parties one time and I had a bunch of these English Lit types standing around me listening to my jokes and I told them this one about the guy who walks into a bar and orders twelve shots of whiskey. The bartender puts them on the bar in front of the guy and the guy starts knocking them back one after the other. The bartender says, "Whoa, fella, you okay?" The guy says, "Yeah, great. I'm celebrating my first blow job." The bartender says, "Hey, that's great! You finish those, I'll get you another whiskey on the house." The guy says, "No, don't bother. If these twelve don't wash the taste out of my mouth, nothing will."

Ba dum bum.

Okay, I am certainly no Cary Grant...or Rodney Dangerfield either.

Now, like I said, I was drunk at that party, but not drunk enough that there wasn't a moment, right before I told that joke, when I asked myself if the subject matter was right for that crowd. The staunch feminist who taught Emily Dickinson and was the University's practicing poet-in-residence was, after all, politely sipping a glass of chardonnay just a few inches from my elbow.

But I told the joke anyway.

I had a similar moment just before I answered my dad's question. My mom, who was so sweet, so pure, and my sister, who was so kickable, were both looking at me expectantly, and my dad, who was so cool, so self-assured, was waiting.

I said, "Randy told me that rattlesnakes form a bolus when they are, uh," I looked up at my mom, then back down at the table, "when they are, uh, trying to making baby rattlesnakes."

Now the way I figure it, I don't think I could have caused a more impressive reaction from all assembled even if I had climbed on top of the table, lowered my pants, and pooped on my dad's plate.

Needless to say, lunch broke up soon after that. My parents had some sort of function they had to go to—functions, I learned early, were the parties where adults went to do business—and after my dad's equivocating answer to my cluster bomb of a question, they couldn't get away fast enough.

On the way downstairs, though, my sister said, "Wow, you sure are slick, you know that?"

"Get lost, Jenny."

"And you've been smoking, too. Haven't you? I can smell it. Where'd you get cigarettes? Did you steal them from Dad? He's gonna kill you if he finds out."

"I didn't steal them from Dad."

"You have been smoking. I knew it."

"I only smoked one," I said.

"Uh huh. I believe that. I should tell Dad. He'd whip your hide till it's raw."

"Leave me alone, Jenny."

She smiled as she slung her scarf over her shoulder. "Suit yourself," she said.

"Jenny, wait!" I said.

I ran over to her. Another of those moments came

and went, another one of those Is-this-really-such-a-good-idea moments. But, young bull that I was, I plowed on.

"What?" she said.

"Jenny, last night…"

"Yeah?"

"I met a girl," I said.

"You met a girl?"

"Yes," I said. "Don't sound so shocked."

She arched her eyebrows at me. "What's her name?"

"Ermelinde."

"Ermelinde," Jenny said rolling the name on the tip of her tongue. "Ermelinde—that's an unusual name. What's her last name?"

"Well, that's the thing," I stuttered. "I didn't get her last name. I was wondering if maybe you knew her."

"I never heard of anybody named Ermelinde—I'd remember a name like that," Jenny said as she left.

Chapter Seven

That night I went down to the lake and sat with my feet over the side of the pier and waited for the girl to come back. I felt sure she would. The night sky was full of stars once more. The moon was full and very large in the sky. It just felt right—the mood, the time, the setting—everything. I thought, "How could she not come on a night like this?"

I called out to her: "Ermelinde."

Her name echoed across the lake. Nothing but silence came back to me. I sat and thought about her, about touching her.

I ended up sitting there for a very long time, waiting. I'm sure I looked pathetic.

Two hours later, I was still sitting there, getting ready to call it a night, when I heard my sister talking. I looked up and saw her coming down the path with the college boy, Cole Prescott, Mr. Yale Phi Beta Kappa. She had both hands around his elbow, and she was giggling about something he'd just said, when she suddenly stopped and waved at me.

"Hey, Mark," she said. "What are you doing, waiting for your girlfriend, the mysterious Ermelinde?"

The two of them erupted in giggles.

I didn't bother with a response.

And then my sister did something totally out of character. She broke away from her latest boy toy and ran towards me, skirts balled in her fist, shoes clacking on the wooden planks of the pier.

I stood up just as she got to me. She was panting from the run.

"What do you want?" I said.

"Don't be like that," she said softly.

Again I didn't bother with a response. I just stared at her and waited. I felt foolish enough sitting around out there in the dark. I didn't need my sister to make me feel like even more of a fool.

She said, "Listen, I asked around about that girl you told me about."

"Yeah?" I tried to keep the interest out of my voice, but I don't think I did a very good job.

"Yeah." She smiled at me, a pretty good imitation

of Mom's sad, sincere little smile. "I'm sorry," she said. "Nobody I've talked to knows her."

She squeezed my hand.

"I really am sorry," she said.

A moment later she was running back up the earthen incline to the main path, where Mr. Stuffed Shirt was waiting, hands in his pockets, the whole world at his feet.

Chapter Eight

My sister's unexpected kindness gave me a second wind of sorts, and I waited down there at the pier for a long time after that. Unfortunately, the girl never showed.

Eventually I started to feel defeated again, like I'd followed the directions on the back of the package to the letter and it still hadn't turned out as promised. I went back to our rented cottage. The lights were off inside, and I figured the family had all gone off to bed.

I walked up the wooden steps to the porch and put my key in the door.

"Where have you been?"

My dad's voice startled me. I turned towards the

porch swing and saw him sitting there, an unlit cigarette in his hand, a faint glint of the moonlight in his eyes.

"Down by the lake," I said.

He struck a match, and for a second, as he touched it to the cigarette he'd put between his lips, I could see his face lit up by an orange glow.

He shook the match out and exhaled smoke.

"You kind of surprised me today." He took a drag off his cigarette. "I thought you had made up your mind to go to the Academy."

I was tired. I didn't want to talk about it with him right then. To be truthful, what I really wanted to do was leave the topic in a permanent holding pattern and hope that it would just go away. I said, "Dad, I—"

"Wave off," he said, meaning don't bother answering. This was him telling me something, not us having a conversation. "I just want you to know, there's never as much time as you think there is. The way you look at the world now, it's like you're shining a flashlight beam into a dark room. You only see this one little spot. There's a lot more out there that you don't see, and if you don't work out a plan now, you're gonna find the rest of the world waltzing right on by you."

That would have been the perfect time for us to have one of those famous father and teenage son fights, but that didn't happen. Instead, before I got a chance to shoot my mouth off, I had a…well, I guess you'd have to call it an epiphany. I looked at my Dad, and instead of seeing somebody who couldn't keep his nose out of my business, I saw a man with a different understanding of the world than the one I had.

I don't mean to say that I suddenly grew up and got a plan for my life. Not by a long shot. It would be years before I had anything close to a plan, and in the end, that plan, when I did finally formulate it, didn't even work out.

No; instead, I realized that my dad didn't see me as a fifteen-year-old kid. What he was looking at was the whole picture, the past, where the boy I used to be was, and the present, where the man I was to become, waited. He saw all of that at once.

At the time I wasn't aware of exactly what he was seeing. I lacked the experience to fully understand it. Now, having looked at my own children in exactly the same way, I've come to think of it as "The Long Look." That look is a parent's complete inability to divorce their own depth of experience from their relationship with their child, and it prevents them from seeing their children as persons who must topple their own obstacles. The Long Look gives you, the parent, the feeling that you can save them the trouble of having to reinvent the wheel. If they'll only do as you say, they can have it so easy. It's like God talking to the Hebrews in Deuteronomy. You tell them over and over again to be good, do as you're told, but it only stays in their heads for a little while.

It is that Long Look that causes so many parents to violate the promises they made to themselves when their children were born that they would never say such things as, "Because I said so" and "Because I'm your father, damn it, and I know what's best for you." I have said both those things—many times, in fact, same as my father said them to me—and I suspect that fathers will go on saying it to their sons ad infinitum ad nauseam as every generation rediscovers the truth that is "The Long Look."

But there is something no parent can predict, no matter how perfect their vision, and that is the pivotal moment, or the sequence of events that make up a pivotal moment, that result in the child becoming an adult. A parent can be a guide during that challenging time, but he or she can never see the event with the same kind of clarity that they see the child's physical body as he grows from infant to adult. That moment, or sequence of moments, is by definition intensely private, and can only be seen from within. I liken it to a wedding. Everyone in the audience knows that you and your bride to be are one thing when you start the ceremony, and something else when the ceremony is over. Everybody knows that the change will take place. But it must be experienced from within for the translation to have meaning.

I understand now that that moment, or sequence of moments, was what my dad was waiting for. That's what he wanted to see, but couldn't. I wish I could have told him that it was coming, because it wasn't far away at all, but I was just as blind as he was when it came to seeing inside myself.

He said, "Will you do me a favor?"

"Of course," I said.

"Will you think about where you want your life to go? Please. It's important."

I watched his face through the drifting curls of smoke from his cigarette and said, "Sure. Yes, sir."

"Good boy." He took another drag, and then put his arms along the back of the swing. "Go to sleep," he said. "We've got a big day tomorrow."

"Yes, sir."

I crept quietly up to my room. I undressed down to my boxers and a T-shirt, then sat at the little pine desk next to my window and looked at the forest on the other side of the driveway.

Butterflies floated through the trees. I watched their erratic, jerky flights, and tried not to think of my future.

And then, suddenly, the girl from the lake was there, standing next to a pine tree, butterflies floating all a-round her hair. She looked up at me and our eyes met.

I jumped to my feet and pressed my face against the glass. She raised one hand, palm up at me, and made a sort of wave.

"Wait!" I said.

I fumbled with the window latch. The window was stuck and I had to fight with it to get it to open. And by the time I did manage to get it open, she was gone. I stuck my head out the window and said, "Hey, wait!" but it was just me, standing there, yelling like a lonely tomcat into the night.

Chapter Nine

Uneasy dreams of Ermelinde again.

I walked through the lonely village again. I saw the daylight pushed back into the corners by an advancing curtain of silvery darkness.

I came to the old church again, the door hanging open, supported by a single hinge, and looked inside.

Ulysses Gaitlin and his kin danced and chanted words that were not English. They were not sane.

On the altar before them was the same woman writhing in the throes of her translation. I heard her moans turn to a mad, stuttering tattoo of barks and yelps before tapering off into a breathy hiss.

I saw the gigantic tail roll in the air. Heard the dull *thwap* of reptilian muscle on the wooden planks. Saw the woman's head and torso rise. And when that gray, misshapen head turned my way, and those round, yellow eyes fixed on mine, regarding me, I turned away and vomited in the street.

I staggered away, and suddenly I was barefoot, I was nude, my feet padding softly in the dark still waters of the graveyard pool.

Ermelinde was swimming naked in the moonlight. As I watched her a gray towering mass of clouds spread across the sky and blotted out the moon. It was dark and cold in the pool and she was gliding out to a small wooden boat in the middle of the water. I watched her move. I seemed to be standing on the bank, though the perspective wasn't right for that.

The world seemed to be clinging to the surface of a soap bubble, wavering somehow, growing closer for a moment then shrinking back with equal suddenness. But despite the dark, and despite the warbling images in front of me, I saw everything with a sharp clarity that made my heart race. Something was wrong. The lines of the skiff seemed too sharp, the colors too vivid.

Ermelinde bobbed up and down in the water by the prow of the wooden boat, and though she hadn't gestured to me or even made eye contact, I felt certain that she knew I was there.

I jumped in and swam across to meet her.

Her chest and tummy were pressed against the prow

of the little skiff.

I put my back against the boat and slid against her wet body, kissing the back of her neck, moving closer, ever closer. My hands worked around to her front and squeezed her breasts—they felt like heaven in my fingers. I kissed her on the side of the neck and she turned towards me. The dark clouds faded away and Ermelinde's face shined in the moonlight—except it wasn't Ermelinde's face anymore. It was the face of a copperhead. Her mouth opened and the sharp fangs sunk into my neck. She grabbed me, but her arms were no longer arms, but more snakes. They kept biting and biting and biting and I woke up with a strange feeling of fear and arousal coursing through my body.

The sheets were soaked with sweat. At least I hoped it was only sweat.

Chapter Ten

The next day started with my sister screaming her lungs out.

We all ran downstairs to see what the problem was. I was still in my boxers and a T-shirt, but I guess my parents were already awake when the commotion started because my dad had shaving cream on his face and my mom was wearing most of her makeup.

"What the hell?" my dad said.

Jennifer was standing against the butcher's block, a shattered glass of milk at her feet.

"What happened?" my dad asked.

"A snake," she said, and pointed at the back patio.

The door was mostly glass, and you could see the patio through it. "Kill it, Daddy."

We all looked where she pointed.

"There's nothing there," I said.

"I saw it," she said. She almost screamed it at me, actually. Sort of a scream and a whine coming out at once.

"Mark," my mom said, "please."

My dad went over to the door and looked out, then he opened it and stepped onto the patio. He looked around a little, then came back inside and shut the door.

"Nothing there," he said. But the way he said it, it was like he was thinking of something else.

"What kind of snake was it?" I asked.

"Mark," Mom said, "please!"

"I don't know," Jennifer said. She was still whining. "It was kind of dusty orange and brown and yellow. God, it was so big. It kept banging its head on the glass, like it wanted to get inside."

"Orange and brown?" Dad asked.

Jennifer nodded into my mom's shoulder, where she had gone for protection.

"Copperhead," I said.

He looked at me and for a horrible moment I thought I saw through his veneer of strength and command to the terrified boy he used to be. But the next moment the window or whatever it was had closed and he was iron once again and I told myself that I was just projecting onto him what I was feeling.

"Yeah, maybe," he said.

"Are those poisonous?" Jennifer asked.

"It's okay, sweetie," my dad said. He touched her hair and then motioned for my mom to get her out of the kitchen.

He turned to me and said, "Mark, help me get this mess cleaned up."

I did as I was told, though I kept thinking about copperhead snakes—the one by the lake, the one that entered the cottage and the ones in my dream.

Chapter Eleven

They used to have a whole category of pulp magazines called spicies. These were the ones you kept separate from your other pulp magazines, maybe hid them
under your mattress, or stuffed them in a shoe box and
kept them behind your baseball glove up on the top shelf
of your closet. I remember titles like *Spicy Mystery* and
Spicy Detective, and there was even a western one called,
predictably enough, *Spicy Western Stories*. Invariably, the
covers featured beautiful women in distress, their
clothes shredded to the point where only a few strate-
gically placed bits of fabric remained, while a bunch of
befeathered African warriors or leering Satanists or crazed
Hindu assassins threatened to do horrible things to them

in the background.

Those magazines had a bad reputation back in the day, but they're fairly tame compared to today's stuff. Hell, I've seen women in my granddaughter's fashion magazines wearing less clothes than some of the spicy covers I remember. But the thing was, if you wanted to read the likes of Robert Leslie Bellem and E. Hoffman Price and Hugh B. Cave, who wrote under the unforgivable pen name of Justin Case when he wrote for the spicies, you had to go to the sauciest of the pulps. There was just no other way around it. And besides, I mean really, what teenage boy wouldn't want his adventure stories to come with a smoking hot platinum blonde who is only a strong breeze away from being totally naked. I mean really. Talk about spot-on marketing.

Well, you can imagine my reaction when, after lunch that day, Randy handed me a brown paper bag and told me to look inside. I pulled out a copy of *Spicy Detective Stories* and saw a blonde whose erect nipples were the only thing holding up a very flimsy towel, a scream suspended on her lips as an unshaven killer in a trench coat and fedora kicked open her bathroom door. There was an R.L. Bellem story advertised on the pages with-in, and a little guilty thrill shot through me.

There were a few more magazines inside the bag.

I slid it back inside the bag and looked around. I felt like a spy trading secrets in the shadow of the Kremlin.

He saw the look on my face and he said, "Yeah, I thought you'd like that."

"Where'd you get those?" I asked.

"Different places. Come on. Let's go down to the gazebo over in the park."

I hesitated. Not because I was afraid of getting caught or anything like that, but because most of the guests were going to be over on the lawn between the clubhouse and the lake and I figured maybe Ermelinde would be there too. That was the day most of the Great Southern Whites descended on the piney woods in the final leg of their Gulf States migration, and everyone was turning out in droves to see it.

I looked towards the lawn and saw about four hundred people milling around, the air around them thick with milky white butterflies. The woods were filled with them before, but now they were like a white wave rolling over the crowd, and I knew from past experience that that wave was only the first of many. Soon they'd be so thick over everything you wouldn't even be able to tell where you'd parked your car. I could hear an excited murmur rising from the crowd, and every once in a while some kid would squeal with delight.

At that moment, Randy's younger brother Ralph showed up at the gazebo. "You aren't supposed to be looking at those naughty magazines. Grandpa says they're full of sin and if you look at 'em you're gonna go straight to hell."

"Shut up, Ralph!" Randy shouted.

"Your grandfather?" I asked.

"Yeah." He looked sullen, but also a little afraid.

"Is he really religious or something?"

"Yeah," he said, "something like that."

"I'm gonna tell Mom," Ralph said.

Randy grabbed his younger brother by the collar and said, "You think you're gonna tell?"

"Yeah," Ralph said. He had a wicked smile on his face.

"You got to get there first, you little shit."

The smile slid off his face and his eyes got big as Randy grabbed him and threw him face down in the grass and rubbed his nose in it.

A couple of grown-ups broke it up a minute or two later and Randy climbed off his brother.

"You keep your mouth closed, Ralph. You hear me?"

Ralph was sniffling, trying to hold back the tears. Without another word he turned and ran off.

I watched him go, feeling nervous. I looked down at the paper sack and thought hard about tossing it. But I guess he read the look on my face because he said, "You're not going to let that little twerp ruin our fun, are you? Come on. Nobody's gonna see. Let's go look at those titties."

Two old ladies in white chiffon summer dresses walked by, trailing butterflies like a bride's train.

"No, I don't think so. Maybe tomorrow."

"What? You're kidding?" A group of kids, maybe ten or eleven, were running through the clouds of butter-flies, laughing like maniacs. We both watched them, and then Randy turned to me like he'd just figured out something. "You're not into that stuff are you? That's lame."

"Another time," I said.

He frowned, but evidently didn't believe I'd already got him behind me.

He pulled out a copy of *Spicy Adventure Stories* and showed me a blonde getting her bra and panties ripped off by an octopus.

"Look at that, man. Can you believe the tits on that girl?"

"They're nice," I admitted, because they were. I didn't bother to ask why a woman would be out in the middle of the ocean wearing nothing but her bra and panties. That seemed beside the point.

"There's this girl named Susan Carlton back at my school, she's got tits like that." He gave me a meaningful look. "I know."

"What do you mean you know?" I knew exactly what he meant of course, but with some people playing dumb is half the fun.

"You know."

"No, I don't know. What do you mean? Did somebody tell you or what?"

His mouth fell open.

"Man, she let me feel her up."

I looked blank.

He looked back expectantly, waiting for the appropriate response. Then he shook his head like he couldn't believe this was happening. "I felt her up."

He cupped his hands in front of him like he was turning on the shower.

I shrugged.

"Are you kidding me? She let me squeeze her tits."

"Oh," I said. Then I frowned. "No, she didn't."

Off on the lawn, the crowd was getting bigger. I could see more people coming down from the clubhouse. Almost everybody was wearing white, which was the custom for this little celebration.

"Yes I did."

"Where at?"

"It was after school. She met me under the fire escape. At first, we just talked, you know? Then she let me kiss her. Then she let me get a hand on those big ole titties. I had to feel them above her shirt. But, you know, a few more kisses softened her up." He gave me a knowing nudge with his elbow.

"Is that it?" I asked.

"No, that wasn't it. After that she let me stick my hands under her shirt, feeling up her bra, then under her bra."

"What did it feel like?"

He smiled. "It was cool."

"So how many tits have you felt, Randy? I mean, besides the numerous roundies beneath your school's fire escape." was having fun with him. I couldn't help it. "Were these particular tits more cool or less cool than other tits. Please enlighten me, O Wise One."

His eyes narrowed. "I bet you never felt up a girl

before," he said.

Like I said, I used to be the young bull, and young bulls like to lock horns, especially when they know they're in the right. A part of me was saying, "Just let it go. Forget about him and move on." But young bulls don't often listen to that voice, especially when the other guy is looking at them the way Randy Worley was looking at me.

"Sure I have," I said.

"Who?"

"You wouldn't know her," I said.

"I might. What's her name?"

I glowered at him.

"Well, what's her name then?"

"You don't know her," was all I could sputter out.

He laughed in my face. "You're a liar. I bet the only tit you've ever seen was your sister putting on her bra or something."

"Knock it off, Randy."

"Or your mom getting out of the bath tub."

I balled my fists. "Take that back."

"Your mom's probably got big old cow dugs—they probably feel all saggy and mushy."

"Take that back, Randy," I warned.

"Stick an egg in the toe of a sock and I could have a tit like hers, too." He put his hands where his nipples were and dangled his index fingers towards the ground and started swinging them back and forth, like a pair of limp, upside down windshield wipers.

"Here you go, boys," he said, prancing around with

his fingers wagging. "Two bags of wet sand. Come and get 'em."

My rage and pent-up frustration was transmuted then into something that felt like a hammer in my hand—and, like Mark Twain so famously pointed out, when you're holding a hammer, every problem looks like a nail.

Long story short, there was a fistfight. A pretty bad one. I don't want to muck this up with a lie and say that I gave him the ass kicking he deserved, because I didn't. I fought pretty well, but so did he, and when it was over, I had a busted lip and a black eye and a dull, aching throb in the back of my head. He had a bloody nose and lips that looked like smashed peaches and a pain in his ribs that kept him from being able to stand up straight.

The whole thing lasted about three or four minutes, but it seemed a lot longer.

Afterwards, he walked off somewhere. I didn't ask where and I didn't care either. I walked in the opposite direction—I wasn't sure where I was going either. I had walked over a hill and there was a fence with a rusty "Do Not Enter" sign in front of it.

I almost ran into Ben Morris, who was picking up trash with his litter stick. He nodded curtly. "Mr. Gaitlin," he said.

"You can call me Mark."

"Hmm," he said. He could see that I have been in a fight, but didn't say a word about it.

Beyond the fence the land bowled upwards to the

tree line. The sky was porcelain blue above us and the pines looked intensely green. Farther in, through the trees, I could see the faint outline of Gaitlinville lost in the lowering shadows.

"Ben?" I asked.

He looked at me. "What happened to calling your elders by their last name?" he said sourly.

An apology rose to my lips instinctively, but I stopped it right at the back of my teeth. He had insulted me, after all. He had insulted my family. I didn't owe him anything.

But I did want answers.

I said, "How do you know so much about my family?"

"I done tol' you. The village up there's a bad place. People round here grow up knowin' it's bad."

"You've never been there," I said. It wasn't a question.

"No, I ain't," he admitted.

"Then how do you know it's bad?"

He took off his litterbag and hung it on the fence and leaned his stick up against the sack. Then he wiped the sweat off the back of his neck with his palm and whipped it off into the grass.

His eyes were yellow, almost jaundiced-looking. Nowadays I recognize that's a sign of advanced hypertension, but at the time it just seemed foreign. There was an air of mystery about him, like one who candidly admits to a belief in superstition.

He said, "You got a haunted house in the fancy neighborhood where you live?"

"A what?"

"You know, an old abandoned place that all the kids like to ride their bikes by and dare each other to go inside, but nobody ever does?"

Now, I grew up in River Oaks, which was, and, as far as I know, still is, Houston's most prestigious neighborhood. There was nothing even remotely close to an abandoned house in my neighborhood. There were pool houses that lay dormant in the winter, but that was as close as it got. Even still, I had been to the movies, and I had read countless pulp rags, and I knew what Ben was trying to say.

I nodded.

"You ever been inside that house?"

I shook my head.

"Then how do you know it's haunted? Why won't you go in it?"

I said, "Because it's got a reputation."

He touched his finger to the tip of his nose.

"Okay," I said, "so tell me the reputation. I didn't grow up around here. What would I know if I did?"

"I done tol' you most of it already," he said. "But I tell you some more. You ever been in Livingston? The town, I mean."

I shook my head.

"Mostly white folks there. They's all poor cotton farmers, but they's still white, and they won't let you forget it."

"You don't live in town?" I asked.

He laughed. "No. I grew up in a little planter's village about three miles down the road. Me and some of the other help, we hitch a ride up here in the morning and hitch a ride home at night. But we don't ever go into Livingston unless we got to call there on business. It ain't a nice place for a black man with nothing in particular to do, if you know what I mean."

"So you live between two bad towns. That's what you're saying?"

"Livingston ain't a friendly place for a black man. There's a difference."

"Okay," I said. "So what's wrong with Gaitlinville?"

"You're making fun, son. This ain't no joke. Where I live they's a lot of scared folks. They know a Gaitlin's come back. There's been signs."

The last part was said with a dark reverence, and I took the bait.

"What kind of signs?"

"Snakes in the street for one. Wilma Sykes done found her hen house swarming with 'em yesterday morning. Copperheads everywhere, she said. And Buster Reese had a sow done dropped a two-headed piglet. This morning I heard the Baptist church in Livingston was covered with crows."

I didn't really know what to think of that. I said, "Okay," and kind of trailed off.

"People say they's sure a Gaitlin done come back

to the lake."

"My family comes back every year," I said. "This is my fourth time here. And you're telling me this is the first time you've had signs?"

"It ain't the first time," he said.

I waited, but he didn't say anything more.

"Oh come on," I said. "You've told me this much. Tell me about the other signs."

"You're making fun again."

"I'm making fun because I have no idea what you're talking about. Now come on, you've told me this much. You wouldn't have said anything at all unless you wanted to tell me the whole thing. Now tell me."

He wiped the sweat from the back of his neck again. Then he looked around, like there might actually be somebody spying on us.

"Like I said, I ain't never been to that village. But my daddy did. Back when he was a boy he did some work for Evan Cullers, who was the postmaster down in Livingston. Even before your great-great-grandfather left, the white folks down there in Livingston wouldn't have nothin' to do with the Gaitlin folks. When they had letters and stuff that needed deliverin', they hire boys like my daddy from the planter's village to carry 'em up there."

"And your dad told you about Gaitlinville?" I asked.

He nodded. "August 13th, 1904. He got paid three cents to take a package of letters up to Gaitlinville. My daddy said when he got there the town was so dead quiet he wouldn't hardly dared to breathe. Said it was completely deserted."

"Deserted," I repeated.

"That's right. Not a soul in sight. The way he tol' me he stepped into that town and it was like the night done swallowed him whole. You could barely see the road for the darkness, even though it was middle of the morning. He was too scared to turn around, too scared to go forward. He just stood there with those letters in his hand. Just stood there shakin' in his shoes."

He paused there, and I said, "That's it? He didn't hear anything? He didn't…see anything?"

Somewhere, back when all this started between us, I had been smiling. I don't remember where or when, but at some point the smile left my face. Now I was standing there, a scared kid, looking at this old black man with nothing short of complete absorption, taking in every detail of his story, every accented syllable, and every pregnant pause.

He looked stricken.

Recognizing that I had him back on the ropes I said, "What did he see in the church?"

That did it. His mouth fell open, and his large, yellow eyes grew round.

I could barely stand myself for my excitement. The dream seemed to be coursing through me now, and surprisingly, it was not a bad thing. I felt certain I knew what his father had seen, and I felt oddly beside myself with a maniacal need to have my dream validated by that young boy's experience.

He looked at me curiously then. And maybe he was afraid.

I don't know for sure. But he scooped up his stick and his bag and said, "I got to get back to work."

"What did he see?" I demanded.

"Nothin'," Ben said. "He dropped them letters and he turned and run home. He didn't see nothin'."

"Bullshit!" I said. "He saw the woman, didn't he? He saw the old gray haired woman turning into a snake, didn't he?"

That stopped him.

He turned and looked at me. His face was ashen with horror.

"You done seen the witch woman, ain't you? You done seen her." He rushed forward and grabbed me by the shoulder.

I tried to shake myself loose from his grip.

"You're hurting me," I said.

He shook me harder.

"You seen her, ain't you?"

"Let go of me," I ordered him.

His expression never changed, but his fingers relaxed. He let one hand fall to his side.

I smoothed out the wrinkles in my shirtsleeves. "Yeah," I said. "I've dreamt about her."

He let go then. "Ah, God," he whispered. Now he was looking from side to side, as though he might see help waiting in the wings somewhere.

"Ben?" I said. "Who is she? Tell me."

"Ah, God," he said again. "It done come again. You gots to promise me, Mark, you gots to stay away from that woman. She's evil."

"Who is she, Ben?"

"She's your kin," he said. "She's the woman who birthed Abraham and Ulysses Gaitlin. Her blood runs through you." He gave me one last look that I can only describe as abject fear, and then he turned and hurried off.

"Ben!" I said.

But it was too late. He was gone.

Chapter Twelve

I went back to the clubhouse, figuring I ought to get cleaned up before I joined my parents out on the lawn, but of course I didn't even make it halfway up the lawn before I ran into my mom. She saw my lip and my eye and the swollen red lumps that had been knuckles half an hour earlier, and she reacted exactly like any other mom would have reacted.

"Oh my God! Mark, oh my God!"

"I'm okay," I said, letting her turn me one-way and then the other as she searched out the scope of my injuries.

When I was nine years old, I had a Schwinn Black

Phantom bicycle. It had the big balloon tires with white-walls, the chrome fenders, deluxe saddle, spring fork, head and tail lights—you name it, it was loaded. It cost twenty-two dollars brand new, and I was king of the neighborhood for the one whole week that I got to ride around on it.

But of course boys will be boys, and one day a bunch of us got together and decided to play polo on our bikes. Bike polo, if you've never played it, is a pretty rough game. We used old baseball bats for mallets and a shred-ded baseball for the ball. You do a lot of sudden stop-ping and changing of direction and even if you're careful, which none of us ever were, you can't help but crash into each other. Your bike takes a beating.

After that game, I hobbled my new, but now irrep-arably damaged bike, home. My mom saw what I had done, and when I lied to her and told her that a car had nearly hit me and caused me to crash my bike, the look of hurt and betrayal on her face was enough to make me feel like I was going to burn in hell for the rest of eternity.

After crashing up my Schwinn and lying about it, my mom had simply gone into the kitchen and talked to the staff about a dinner party she was hosting that weekend, leaving me with just my guilt and lack of bicycle as punishment. My father, I'm pretty sure, never heard anything about it.

Remembering that, I decided to tell her the truth. Or at least most of the truth. Casting my eyes to the ground, I told her that I had been in a fight—though I didn't tell her why. They say telling the truth is supposed to make it better. It didn't. Though I told the truth, the feeling in my gut was the same as when I told the lie about the bike. It seemed awfully unfair to me.

There was a smoldering silence between us.

My mother's anger swelled the longer the silence went on, but instead of shaming me into submission, which may or may not have been her intention, all I could do was think of a joke I'd once heard my dad tell at a party. Jesus went into a village and found a crowd gathered around a woman, preparing to stone her to death. Jesus stood in front of the woman and said: "Let anyone here without sin cast the first stone." A stone flew from the crowd, over Jesus' shoulder, and hit the woman square in the face. Jesus looked at the stone-thrower and exclaimed, "MOTHER!"

Ba dum bum.

My comedy was turning against me.

"Go back to the cottage—right this very moment," she said. When she got angry she hardly ever yelled. When she was really angry, she seethed, the words coming out like steam escaping from deep in the guts of a machine, quiet but ominous.

But Ermelinde, I thought. She could be out there.

"Mom, everybody's gonna be out on the lawn. You wouldn't want me to miss the…"

She wasn't going to be swayed this time.

"You're gonna talk to your father about this." She

started to say more, but she was too angry to get the words out. "My God, Mark. What's gotten into you? Fighting in public, I expected more from you." Her voice had dropped to a barely audible hiss. "It's disgusting."

I looked past her at the crowds, at all the shining, happy faces in the sunlight, laughter and butterflies filling the air, and a wave of anxiety flooded over me. She could be out there, and I'm missing her.

"Mom," I said, and tried to give my voice that same imploring tone that I'd given her that first night, the night she let me leave the dance.

She looked away from me.

"Don't talk to me right now," she said. "Just go back to the cottage. I don't want to see you right now."

And then she walked away.

Chapter Thirteen

I half expected my dad to come home and kick my ass. That's what I would have done if it'd been me who had to take time off from all the excitement to come back home and deal with a smart-assed kid who had just run his mother's trust through the mud.

But, surprisingly enough, that didn't happen.

"Let's take a walk," he said, and led me outside. There wasn't a trace of anger in his voice.

We stepped onto the red dirt path that led from our back patio up into the pine forest. Butterflies fluttered across the path and filled the shadows beneath the trees with movement.

As we walked I thought about what I was going to say, how I was going to explain myself. I'm sorry, Dad, but that Randy Worley, he kept teasing me. He wouldn't stop. What would you have done? I couldn't just stand there and take it.

I figured some variation of that, repeated over and over again, would eventually mollify him, just like my mom's anger would eventually fade too.

The thing was, I was troubled. And it wasn't because I had only told my mom most of the truth. It was why the fight had started in the first place that bothered me. Randy had crossed the line by bringing my mother into it, but that wasn't the only reason we fought. Hell, it wasn't even the main reason. The thing that really bothered me was that I had lunged at him, really laid into him with all the rage and muscle I had, because he didn't believe the girl from the lake existed, that what had happened between her and me had really happened. That was what did me in. That was what put me over the edge. It was like he was taking her away from me by not believing me, and that made me crazy mad.

I suppose I could have spared myself a little of my mom's fury by telling her that Randy had made a crack about her. I could have said something Quixotic, like "No guy's gonna let a punk like Randy talk bad about his mom. That's why I had to fight him, Mom. I had to. Your honor demanded it."

I probably would have left off the part about her honor demanding it, but you get the idea. And it probably would have earned me a smile. It certainly would have been better than the look I did get from her.

"You know, I came here once before," Dad said. "When I was sixteen. With your grandfather."

He had picked up a twig and was picking the bark off it with his thumbnail as we walked.

I shook myself out of my thoughts and said, "I remember you telling me that."

"That's right, I did, didn't I."

He got a big piece of the bark loose, and then he tried to tell me something important.

"My mom—your grandmother—died the September before. Your grandfather and I…God we were a mess after that. That first Christmas Day after she died, we both sat at the kitchen table and stared out the back window till almost noon.

Neither of us even bothered to look at the tree."

He tossed the twig into the shadows.

"Dad wasn't making a lot of money back then, but he pooled together what he had and he brought me here. That summer we watched the butterflies come in through the pines. It was the same then as it is now. Very beautiful, and that is why I bring the family here now. This place, it can be beautiful."

He was trying to find a way to say what he had to say, so I stayed quiet. I let him search for it in his own time.

"I'm not explaining this very well. I'm sorry. There's so much to this, Mark. Your grandfather, that abandoned village up there, our name's all over this place. Our family has a tie to this land that…Does it call to you too, Mark? It calls to me. This lake, I…something happened here. To me, I mean. On that trip."

Again I waited.

"I look back on that trip…on what happened, I mean, and I…Ah, hell. I just think of the choices, those damn choices you make in life. The wrong ones, they haunt you in the middle of the night."

He was stammering badly, not at all the silky-voiced scholarly attorney whose brain was like a dictionary with three languages readily on tap that I had grown up with—and I didn't know why. Though in my own obtuse way I could tell he was trying to reveal some great failure of his.

We slowed to a crawl, like two monks in meditation walking beneath the colonnade of a cloister between afternoon prayers. I waited for him to open whatever wounds were there in him. I was very much aware that, for whatever reason, I was getting this glimpse into his past, and it had nothing whatsoever to do with disciplining me for fighting.

"I look back on that vacation," he said, and this time his voice sounded surer, his thoughts more in order, "and the best way I can describe it to you is to compare it to a buoy at sea. It's like, on this side of the buoy, you've got the shallow water, the familiar. But beyond it, you've got the deep water. When I look back on that trip, I see this lake that way, like the buoy that marks the point where life got complicated." He shook his head. "It's hard to be more exact than that without robbing you of something."

He smiled at me. I tried to smile back.

"What happened here, Dad?"

"Listen," he said, "I want you to promise me something."

"Okay."

"I want you to promise me that if you see a chance to do something wonderful, something really great, that you won't back away from it—no matter what happens. You have to listen to your heart, your brain and your soul. Sometimes your heart will be telling you something, but your brain and soul will tell you something else. But if you've got to choose, choose your heart. You'll never go wrong. Never. Promise me you'll do that, won't you—Mark?"

I had no idea what he was talking about. But there was an intense look in his eyes when he stared at me that made me feel both profoundly humble and kind of creeped out at the same time. He wanted me to understand something important, and I wanted to understand it. I really did.

When your father looks at you that way, it can be a life-altering experience. And it makes me think of that joke again, the young bull and the old bull standing on the hillside. I wonder if, after the punch line, the younger bull had some sort of epiphany. Did he realize that the keys to the kingdom were being placed around his neck?

"Dad," I swallowed hard. "I will try not to let you down."

But before he could answer, I grabbed his arm and pulled him back. He was wearing a white suit and white leather shoes. He crinkled his brow at me, and his face looked very yellow against all that white. Then his gaze followed to where I was pointing, and his eyes went wide.

Skeins of pine needles had worked their way onto the red dirt path ahead of us, and there, in the middle of one of those skeins, just inches from the toe of his white leather shoe, was a four-foot long copperhead, to this day one of the biggest I have ever seen.

He made a startled-sounding guffaw and took a quick step back. When he looked at me there was a big thank you in his eyes and he was breathing hard.

We both took a few more steps back, never looking away from the snake.

It surprised us both, I think, when the copperhead unfolded itself and slithered towards us. My dad put out his arms and started flapping them. I thought maybe he was having a heart attack or a stroke. I grabbed my dad to hold him up, and I could feel every muscle in his body trembling.

The snake kept coming towards us.

I picked up a rock and threw it at the snake, missed it by mere inches, and it slithered in the other direction.

The experience he had been trying to relate to me was lost, the moment gone. It wouldn't return for more than sixty years—until three months ago, actually—when he told it to me from his deathbed in San Antonio's Methodist Transplant and Specialty Hospital.

Chapter Fourteen

Let me tell you what East Texas is like in the summer. It is unbearably hot. It is unbearably humid. The heat will crumple you like a dropped pair of pants. You sleep in your underwear and you kick the covers all the way down to the foot of the bed in the vain hope that when you wake up the sweat won't have glued you to the sheets.

Everyone else was at the dance, the big end of the week the butterflies-have-finally-come dance. It was nine, nine-thirty at night. I was in bed, in my underwear, the sheets kicked down to the foot of the bed, trying to focus on an Elmore Leonard story called "Only Good

Ones" in the latest issue of *Roundup* and not doing a very good job of it.

Though night had fallen, the heat was still powerful, and I could smell the odor of baking pine needles coming through my open window. My mind was wandering, and I read the same exchange of dialogue three times before I finally tossed Elmore Leonard back into my suitcase, laced my hands together behind my head, and stared up at the ceiling to think about my dad.

East Texas was a hot, humid hell in the summertime, but my dad had given this vacation its own microclimate. It was odd. I felt protected by the security he had provided for me and my family, the wealth his legal acumen and political savvy had put between us and a rapidly changing world, and yet at the same time I was confused. I felt that I had known and understood the man just a few days prior to seeing The Long Look in his eyes, and then there had been his enigmatic injunction that I wouldn't back away from the opportunity to do something really great, and suddenly I was drifting, not sure at all whether I would ever be able to understand what he was about.

There was a pop at the window.

I looked that way and didn't see anything. Everything was as it should have been. The white curtains moved sluggishly in the breeze. And then, as I watched, I saw a flash of something small, a rock or a small clod of dirt strike the window frame with another pop sound.

I got out of bed and crossed to the window. I half-expected to see Randy Worley down there, either ready for round two or willing to put it all behind us.

Either way, I knew what I was going to tell him.

But it wasn't Randy. It was Ermelinde. She was standing there on the path where she had been a few nights earlier, looking up at me and smiling. Her hair was the color of iced tea. Her eyes flashed in the moonlight. Her dress clung to her body in all the right places —she looked just as good in that summer dress as she did swimming nude in the lake.

I leaned out the window. "Hi," I said.

She smiled. Butterflies swarmed all around her.

"You out for a walk?" I said, and groaned inwardly at my complete lack of cool. I made myself a promise right then to watch every Cary Grant movie ever made in the desperate hope that at least some of his smoothness would rub off on me.

Ermelinde gestured for me to come down.

"I'm kind of grounded," I said.

Her smile melted into a pout—just like the one she had given me that first night when I hesitated before taking off my boxers.

"I'll get in a lot of trouble."

She turned to walk away.

"Wait!"

She stopped.

"What's a little trouble, right?"

There was that smile again.

"Hang tight," I said, thinking: What's the worst that

could possibly happen? "I'll be right there."

I dressed in a hurry, choosing black slacks and a white collared shirt. I decided to go for the untucked look and right before I ran down stairs, I put my hands in my pocket and looked at myself in the mirror, sticking my lower lip out slightly in my best Robert Mitchum impression. Robert Mitchum I could do. I had the same cheek structure and sleepy-looking eyes.

These are the clothes you were wearing the night you lost your virginity, I told myself, and gave my reflection a wink.

Then I flew down the stairs like an Olympic sprinter. I went out the back door and trotted up to the path where I had seen her, but she wasn't there.

"Hey," I called out. "Where are you?"

She was standing in the front yard, motioning for me to follow. When I started towards her, she turned and started walking towards the path that led from the row of cottages down to the lake.

"Hey," I said. "Wait up."

I jogged after her until I caught up.

"Where you going?" I asked. "Everybody's down at the clubhouse. If you want, we've got the house to ourselves."

Ermelinde shook her head no.

"I'm sorry," I said, embarrassed. "We can go wherever you want."

She smiled again.

I was determined not to repeat my mistake from

the night we met, grabbing her breasts like I did. If she didn't want to go into the house with me, maybe it was because it made her nervous, like she'd be trapped in there with no way out if she changed her mind. She wanted to be somewhere where she felt more at ease, more in control of what happened. I could understand that. I mean, I was the young bull, sure, but I was also brought up to be a gentleman. I remember, right before I left for my first date, my dad gave me the only sex talk I ever got from my parents. He said, "You just remember, you are responsible for everything that happens to that girl from the moment she leaves her house to the moment she walks back in it. And you better behave accordingly."

Those words stayed with me all right, and they flashed through my head as I trailed along slightly behind that girl, watching her hips move up and down under her thin rust-colored dress. It didn't look like she was wearing panties.

"So where are we going?" I asked. "You want to go down to the lake, do a little swimming maybe?"

She shook her head no again.

"Okay."

I was determined not to scare her off, so I kept my mouth shut.

We walked across the little park that was between the guest cottages and the lake, found a sort of towpath next to the water, and made our way towards the pier.

"So what's your last name?" I asked. "I know your

first name and you know my name, but I never got your last name."

Without stopping or even slowing down, she put her finger over my lips and shushed me with her eyes. Her touch was electric, and for a second it took my breath away. I slowed down until I was almost standing still. I have read stories where people talk about how some event suddenly snapped their mind into focus, how it felt like every nerve was on fire with the sensation of being alive, and I always thought that was mere hyperbole, an inevitable side effect of paying hack writers a penny a word. But what happened to me when she touched her finger to my lips was exactly like that. The world as I knew it just fell away. I watched the grass beneath my shoes move with an insect-like speed. I leaned my head all the way back and stared at a cloud passing overhead. It rumbled like a mountain falling into the sea.

"Whoa," was all I was able to get out.

I was swaying like a drunk. Her touch had done something to me that I still, to this day, don't understand. I was floating, but at the same time, hyperaware of even the most minute sensory input. I could hear the roar of butterfly wings. I could feel the dust in the breeze touching my skin. Every beat of my heart was an explosion in my chest. My lips were trembling.

It was hard to focus, but I saw the girl walking away from me, towards the piney woods. She was a good thirty yards ahead of me. Beyond her, the lawn sloped upwards like the inside of a bowl towards the tree line. She didn't turn to see if I was still with her. She just walked on, her pace easy.

I staggered after her.

Now I love my wife. I have loved her for all forty-three years of our wonderful marriage. And I loved her for the two years we dated before that. Ours is a love that grew steadily. It took hold during late night study sessions during the spring semester of our junior year at The University of Texas at Austin, and gradually, as we came to know each other better, our friendship blossomed into love.

During the nearly half a century that we have been together, my wife has worn many perfumes. I have known her in the drugstore cheap stuff that was all I could afford to buy her during my law school days, and I have known her in the liquid gold French-made stuff that I have money enough to buy her by the bucket these days; but for all the money those perfumes cost, I have never known those scents to intoxicate me the way I felt that night heading into the piney woods.

Even from a distance I could smell that girl, and yet it wasn't a smell that you could recognize. It affected me on a deeper level than my senses were capable of reaching. I could feel it spreading inside me, attaching to my body on a biochemical level that was like I had just uncovered that thing that had been missing from my existence and now I desperately had to make it mine.

That makes no sense, I know. But I submit that it

doesn't have to. Perhaps it can be explained by phero-mones or something like that, though I don't think that matters. The heart is crazy when it needs what it needs. I know only that her scent kept me crashing headlong into the underbrush, pushing my way through twigs and briars and dense, sap-covered thorny vines with complete abandon. The skin of my arms and hands and neck and face that had just moments ago been able to feel the air rippled by a butterfly's wing was now oblivious to the vegetation that was ripping me to shreds.

And still Ermelinde moved along ahead of me, her scent like a cold channel in a river for me to follow.

But she did not stop. The path opened up beneath our feet and became more like a road. I could see the ghostly outlines of Gaitlinville ahead of us, black and si-lent in the shadows.

"Wait for me," I said, pleading with her, really.

She turned her head just enough to show me her beckoning smile.

"How much farther?" I asked.

I wanted her to touch me again. I wanted the full charge that was in her to pass through to me. Quick-ening my pace I tried to catch up with her, but she always stayed ahead of me. Even when I nearly broke into a run, she stayed ahead of me. And yet she never appeared to change her pace at all. It was always an easy, graceful step through the trees.

And then suddenly we were in the little abandoned village. I looked up at the sky wheeling above me. Then down at the silent village, the girl walking off into the gloom near the church. The buildings shone with a lustrous silvered glow, the empty, doorless doorways leered at me, and it seemed to me that something moved there in the shadows, driven mad by its loneliness.

"Please stop," I called after her.

I stumbled forward. We crossed the street and passed the church, walked through the little cemetery and out to the wilderness beyond.

Though my head was still reeling I could make out a dark pool of water ahead of her, and somewhere in the back of my mind I knew that whatever it was that we were moving towards was there. I could feel it in the air like an electrical charge. I knew she would stop there.

She slipped her dress over her head and walked naked into the water, moving away from the edge of the pool until she was neck deep.

And there she stopped.

I stood on the shore, watching her. The water was green and glowing, as though lit from within.

She turned and said, "Come inside with me, Mark."

Her hands were open, palm up on the surface of the water before her. I stood there, swaying, my mouth dry.

"Come inside with me, Mark," she said.

"I...I'm afraid."

"There's nothing here to hurt you," she said.

Her voice was a clear bell in the fog. She was heat,

and my body craved warmth.

My father's words rose up in my mind. Listen to your heart. It won't lead you astray.

"No," I said softly.

"Mark, come to me."

I was a marionette being led about by my strings. I pulled at my shirt, at my belt. My clothes fell away and a moment later I was stepping into the pool, naked.

I waded over to her and stopped, facing her, my lips trembling.

A copperhead broke the plane of the water and its head passed within an inch of my chin. The slow, undulating curves of its body pressed against my cheek. I could feel its need to rub its body on mine, to press itself up against my skin.

More snakes emerged from the water and pressed against me, wrapping around my legs and arms. Around my waist. Still more were sliding into the murk from the pool's muddy banks. I looked about, my heart in my throat, abject terror pushing inward through the haze in my brain. Soon the entire pond was a writhing mass of snakes.

I was shaking badly, muttering gibberish.

"Shhh," she said, her fingers dancing across my cheek. Her touch settled me. The beating of my heart didn't hurt quite so badly.

But down through the darkness of the frothing water I could see a thick mass of snakes entwining me, rubbing against me. They were a bolus, a rotating ball of muscle, their heads breaking the surface for a moment here and there and then ducking back under again so frequently that the sound reminded me of the quiet patter of raindrops in puddles. One glided onto my outstretched arm and shot up towards my face. It turned away at the last moment and its bulk slapped against my cheek. Fear overwhelmed me and I began to scream. I screamed until every last ounce of me was contained in that sound. And when there was nothing left, I broke down and sobbed. Every contact, every touch, made me flinch. "I don't want to die," I said, and the tears fell one after another until those too sounded like raindrops falling into puddles.

I raised my eyes from the swirling mass around my body and saw the girl ahead of me. Her smile was that of a woman completely aroused, lips parted, eyes shining. She ducked her head towards the water and in one liquid motion she changed. Her body fell forward into the water without a splash. Her legs curled upwards and backwards, sloughing away as they broke the surface to reveal a long, undulating length of glistening snakeskin.

She was gliding towards me then, a four-foot-long copperhead with a cold intelligence in her eyes. There was a purpose there, a need.

She glided up to me and her face hovered inches from my face. I looked into those eyes and I knew that I did not want to be her mate or her consort or any other thing that had anything to do with what she was and what was happening to me. I knew more than anything else in the world I wanted to be gone from there.

I closed my eyes and said, "Get away get away get away! Please. Get away."

A sort of yellow, soapy foam had risen from the water all around me. It smelled foul. The girl, for I could still see the girl inside the snake, glided around my left shoulder and wrapped around the back of my neck. I could feel her excitement. The smell was doing something to her, calling forth her denning instincts, compelling her to press her snake flesh against my human flesh, creating friction and heat.

I don't know what sort of dumb luck preserved me, but something was looking out for me that night in the piney woods. I scrambled out of that soapy, scummy water and landed on the bank of that little pool, and I did it without getting a single bite—at least not from the bolus that had entwined me in its mass. I can think only that I was under Ermelinde's protection.

Or perhaps I had enraged her to the point that the others dared not get between us.

Coughing and shaking, every inch of me wet with mud and filthy water, I pulled myself up to my hands and knees and crawled away from the pool. I don't know how long it lasted—though it couldn't have been more than a second or two—but there was a moment when I felt like I was in the clear.

But I wasn't. Water dripped from my nose and plopped into the dirt. I watched a few drops fall, and when I looked up, Ermelinde was there in front of me, head moving, bobbing on the air a foot or so off the ground.

I scrambled to one side and tried to flank her, but in her snake form she was faster, moving to stay in front of me. She was trying to force me back into the water, back into that writhing mass of muscle that was the bolus. I could see her intentions in her eyes.

"No," I said. "No!"

The snake came forward. I jumped backwards, kicking at her, trying to keep her head away from my legs, but she was faster than I was.

"Stop it!" I screamed. "I don't want to. Stop it!"

She bolted forward and bit me in the calf. She bit me on the thigh, and once more on the hand before I could pull myself away.

I flinched. I twisted and screamed with everything I had, but this time in pain rather than in fear.

Ermelinde started shedding her snakeskin, and her human form climbed up from the limp shell of scales and stood on bare feet. I looked up and saw her girl's body changing, the hair turning gray, the breasts sagging, creased with wrinkles. The old woman from my dream stood before me.

I heard the faint chanting from my dream again, a low sibilant hiss that I couldn't understand.

Her old woman hips swayed to the slow, Skeltonic beat of her chanting, and she came closer, reaching for me.

"No," I said, falling backwards.

The venom from her bites was coursing through me, and I could feel an icy ring of numbness forcing its way under my skin.

My legs felt heavy and I couldn't move.

She dropped down onto her hands and pulled herself toward me with a sickening, slithering motion. I closed my eyes and cried.

"Please, God, no," I said. "Please."

Then she let out a shriek of pain that echoed off the trees.

I opened my eyes. She was convulsing wildly, twisting around to reach the litter stick that was poking out of her back. Ben appeared beside her and grabbed the litter stick and jammed it deeper into her, the look on his face a deranged mix of fear and hate and bloody rage.

She rolled over, twisting the white of her bare belly over him and throwing him to the ground. Her body seemed to wrap around him, squeezing him. I could see contractions riding up her flanks as she pressed against him, trying to loosen his grip.

But Ben fought her. He slowly worked his feet under him until he had the leverage to stand, and when he regained his feet, he jammed the litter stick down into her once again.

The woods filled with her shrieks.

She let go her grip on him and he staggered backwards.

"Fucking bitch," he hissed, and pulled a huge five-inch lock blade from his back pocket. He clicked it open, then advanced on her, holding her head by her hair as he sawed the head from her body.

I watched the body twitch helplessly in the mud. I looked towards the severed head hanging from the tangled gray hair in Ben's fist. I watched the expression on her face twist, the life slowly ebbing from her eyes, the mouth going slack, and falling open to reveal the fangs within.

Ben tossed the head into the pool and we both watched it sink, the snakes sliding in after it.

"Can you stand?" Ben asked.

His face swam before me.

"I can't feel my legs," I said.

He nodded. Then he picked me up and carried me out of the ruins of Gaitlinville.

Chapter Fifteen

I became a corporate lawyer because I still have a lisp from the poisoning I got that night, and a trial lawyer with a lisp is like a bikini model with only one breast: it doesn't matter how nice the rest of her is, people aren't going to pay attention to that.

I also walk with a limp, something about irreparably atrophied muscle in the thigh, I'm told.

They told me I was lucky to be alive. Believe me, they made sure I knew that. Ben carried me out of the woods and down to the resort's office. It must have been quite a sight, an old black man carrying a nearly comatose, and completely naked, white kid down from the woods.

Luckily I wasn't conscious for that part of the conversation. I do remember shocked voices, frantic foot-steps in and out of the room, a woman—my mom, no doubt—screaming. The room faded in and out. An old, grandfatherly-looking man leaned over me, pried my eyelids up with his fingers, and said, "Snake bite. He's in shock."

The man was Dr. George Herbert, who was, in his day, Houston's finest heart surgeon. So I guess I was pretty lucky at that.

I was stabilized and taken to a hospital, where I dreamt fevered dreams.

It took me about two weeks to get to the point where I could walk around on my own. Once again I heard how lucky I was to be alive. And when my mom and sister heard that, oh brother the pampering I did receive! Dad also popped in from time to time, and once, in the middle of the night, I woke and saw him sleeping in the chair next to my bed, a paperback edition of Mark Twain's *Roughing It* spread open over his chest. I went back to sleep thinking how nice it was to have people willing to take care of me.

My parents never questioned me as to why I disobeyed them and left the house that night. Not directly, anyway. Bit by bit, I told them a toned down version of the story, how I had gone to the clubhouse for something to eat, and then gone into the woods because I thought I heard somebody calling for help. It was there, while roaming the woods looking for that lost soul, that I was nearly lost myself.

I left out the part about the girl.

And they never mentioned my lack of clothes. That, I think, they chalked up to delirium and the hallucinatory effects of envenomation.

My mother believed it, I'm sure. I think after the grounding she gave me for the fight, and then seeing me on that picnic table in the resort's back room, she would have believed anything I told her—as long as it meant having me alive.

But my father was another matter. When he heard my watered down version of events, he gave no reaction at all. Our eyes met and held, and I could have sworn he was trying to tell me something.

Chapter Sixteen

My mom died of breast cancer in September of 1986. My father, like I've said already, died three months ago. Not from throat cancer, surprisingly, or even heart disease, though he smoked until the day we brought him to the hospital. No, it was the prostate cancer bullet that eventually got him.

My sister is alive and well, and living with her second husband in Pennsylvania. They have a lovely country place near Pittsburgh, very close to where they filmed the original *Night of the Living Dead*, a little bit of local history of which she is not very proud. She never did share my love of pulp, poor thing. Used to be, just to goad her, I'd call her up and in my best creepy guy voice say, "They're coming to get you, Jennifer." It was a running joke between us for a long time, though I haven't done it in years. Maybe I'll call her this evening.

I have no idea what happened to Randy Worley, though sometimes I like to imagine that he's dying of dysentery in the bowels of a Mexican jail. One can only hope, right?

Old Ben slipped into the past unnoticed—and probably unthanked for pulling my stones out of the fire. I never heard anything about what happened to him. Maybe this summer I'll go into Livingston and see if I can find out where he's buried.

These days, Lake Livingston is a sportsman's paradise. They built a dam there in 1966 and flooded most of the surrounding piney woods, so that today the lake takes up something like 93,000 acres and offers full service marinas and waterside restaurants and fifteen million dollar summer mansions. It's an easy car trip from both Houston and Dallas, so you're as likely to see beautiful girls in tiny bikinis sunning themselves on the decks of million dollar yachts as you are drunken rednecks fishing the weed-choked shallows from their fifteen-foot Renegade flat bottoms. It is, from all I've heard, nothing at all like the secluded quiet retreat I knew in my youth.

To this day I receive a copy of the Sunday edition of the *Livingston Daily Star*, just on the offhand chance of catching a story about a young man who has been attacked by a copperhead.

Chapter Seventeen

Ten months after my envenomation, my dad took me golfing for the first time. I think it pleased us both, that round of golf. My dad because he got to spend some quality man-to-man time with his son, and me because I learned that my snake-bit bum leg wouldn't forever keep me out of all sporting events. Baseball, football, those were out. But not golf. I picked up a lifelong passion that day.

Afterwards, Dad took me for a root beer float. We sat in a booth in the little mom and pop pharmacy near our house and he smoked while I dug the vanilla ice cream out of the glass with a spoon.

"You mind if I ask you a personal question?" he said.

"Sure, Dad." I put my spoon back into the glass. "What do you want to know?"

"It's about the night that you—" he pointed at my leg and sort of rolled his hand around in a vague circle that was supposed to say, 'You know'—"the night you …well, you know, got bit."

"Yeah?"

"You said you heard somebody crying in the woods."

"Yeah?" I said, my voice edged with caution that I couldn't quite disguise.

"Was it a man or a woman's voice?"

"I couldn't tell," I said.

He didn't say anything to that, and the silence made me nervous. "It was too far away," I said, just to fill up that silence.

He took a last drag from his cigarette, exhaled, and then crushed it out, his eyes on mine the whole time.

"You didn't see anybody else out there?"

I swallowed the lump in my throat, and then I shook my head.

"Nobody?" he asked.

"Nobody," I said.

Chapter Eighteen

You know, for the last sixty years, I thought this was a story about me coming of age. And it is, really, though not in any sort of traditional way. I mean, there was the time of innocence before that trip. And then there was the unreal moment when I stood in that piney forest pond and my horizons were pushed far beyond the limited understanding I had enjoyed up to that point. And finally, there was my return to this world, my outlook forever changed. Innocence, adventure, returns with new knowledge. Those elements are, by definition, the key plot points in a coming of age story—at least that's the way I understand it from the Joseph Campbell that I've read.

But the thing is, for as big as all that is, it's only part of the picture. It is the meat of the tale, but not its true significance, not its flavor. Coming of age stories are like shouts into a canyon. They should echo. If they don't carry over into the new person who emerges from the trials of the adventure, if they don't destroy the boy and rise up a man in his place, then there's no point in having the adventure in the first place.

Coming of age is the most intensely personal experience imaginable, and, ironically, the most public. I mean, it's no secret or anything. We all know that people are born children and become adults somewhere along the line. We can all look at our peers and see who has learned life's lessons and who has learning still to do. But the actual act of coming of age is, ultimately, a personal one. It is an inward journey. And no one can do it for you. No one can hand you a book and say, "Here is what it means to come of age. Like Holden Caulfield or David Copperfield. Understand what this book says and you will be able to avoid the pain of experiencing it for yourself."

In other words, you can have as many guides as you like, but in the end, you're on your own.

That day in the pharmacy, when my dad asked me all those questions, I thought I had the situation figured out. I don't mean to say that I could have explained it to him—at least not in the clear, concise language he taught me. The experience was in my mind like a word that's stuck on the tip of your tongue. You know what you want to say, but you just can't get it out.

Much later, as I got far enough away from the experience to see the whole of it, I came to realize that even then, sitting in that pharmacy booth across from my dad, eating a root beer float, I sensed that what happened to me in those woods was intensely personal, that I alone owned it. Not even Old Ben could claim all of it. Not in the same sense that I could. That was my moment, my coming of age moment, and though others might be able to feel the aftershock of that moment, only I could see it from the inside out.

I think that was the reason why I lied to him about seeing the girl. Of course he wouldn't have believed me had I been stupid enough to tell him about the girl turning into a snake.

Thinking back on it, my reasons for keeping quiet about her were exactly opposite from my reasons for fighting with Randy. When Randy told me I was a liar, it felt like he was robbing me of this wonderful thing. And yet, with my dad, it felt like the only way to keep that wonderful thing wonderful was to remain silent about it.

Realizing that I was happier keeping the experience private convinced me, more than anything else, that I really had had a coming of age moment. The experience in and of itself was sufficient. I didn't need any outside affirmation to give it worth.

Chapter Nineteen

My dad was lucid to the end. He was in tremendous pain, but he was always lucid. He had taken to wearing his hair slicked back again, the way he had when I was a kid, and I remember sitting next to his bed and smelling his hair gel and being transported back across decades to those summers we spent at Lake Livingston.

One day, right before he died, I was sitting in the chair next to his bed, joking with him. My sister got up to get us some Cokes from the cafeteria several floors down, and I noticed my dad watching her back as she left the room.

I sensed a change in his demeanor, like he was waiting for her to be out of earshot before he said what he wanted to say.

I waited.

When she was gone, he turned to me and said, "Tell me the truth, Mark."

"I'm sorry?" I got the feeling he had started the conversation in his head before joining it with me.

"The girl at the lake. The one you followed out into the woods."

My guess is that all the color drained out of my face, because he saw through me right away. He saw whatever it was he expected to see, then smiled and fell back into his pillow. He was winded from the effort.

Now imagine this. Imagine an experience that means everything to you, one that for sixty years you believed was yours alone. Imagine that the person you are today has taken strength from that experience, that it is your private psychological foundation, your rock. It is the lens through which you understand yourself and your relationship with the people you love.

Now imagine that in one fateful moment, late in life, you realize that you had completely misunderstood the importance of that event. Imagine the magnitude of that psychological earthquake.

I have been thinking an awful lot about the past since my father died, and I've come to the opinion that the past is a very dangerous thing. You can sit on the pier and dangle your toes into the water of the past, and you might even think it's rather pleasant, but if you get in and swim around in it, you can very quickly lose yourself.

"That day we walked together in the woods behind our cottage," Dad said. "Remember that?"

"Yes," I said. My voice was dry and brittle, and though I tried to quiet it, there was a tremor there as well.

"I wanted to tell you then, but I lost the nerve. I wonder what would have happened had I told you."

"Told me what, Dad? What are you talking about?"

"The girl you saw in the woods, the one who led you out into the woods..." He broke off there, groaning from the pain in his groin.

"How do you know about her, Dad?"

He smiled tiredly.

"I saw her that time your grandpa and I went to the lake. I had a chance to follow her, and I got scared. I didn't do it. I always wondered what would have happened, what kind of man I would have been had I not refused her call."

I tried to get more out of him, but he wouldn't say anything else. He just kept repeating over and over again that things might have turned out differently.

He died a few days later.

Since the funeral, I've mulled it over again and again. For my dad, I think the experience was one of intense failure, and that failure haunted him the rest of his days. It was the whip at his back as he climbed the ladder of professional accomplishment.

For me, the experience was exactly the opposite. I

have never felt the need to feed in the frenzy that is the corporate world. There is no whip at my back. Outwardly, I have never been the success that my dad was. But I have lived at peace with myself, and isn't that the single greatest success we can ever hope to achieve?

I wonder now if my dad was aware of that. Did The Long Look extend that far? Did he really lose the nerve to tell me about his failure to answer the call, or did he intentionally hold himself back so that I would have the chance to attain that peace?

It makes me wonder who really had the clearer understanding of the event we seem to have both shared.

ABOUT THE AUTHORS

Joe McKinney has his feet in several different worlds. In his day job, he has worked as a patrol officer for the San Antonio Police Department, a DWI Enforcement officer, a disaster mitigation specialist, a homicide detective, the director of the City of San Antonio's 911 Call Center, and a patrol supervisor. He played college baseball for Trinity University, where he graduated with a Bachelor's Degree in American History, and went on to earn a Master's Degree in English Literature from the University of Texas at San Antonio. He was the manager of a Barnes & Noble for a while, where he indulged a lifelong obsession with books.

He published his first novel, *Dead City*, in 2006, a book that has since been recognized as a seminal work in the zombie genre. Since then, he has gone on to win two Bram Stoker Awards and expanded his oeuvre to cover everything from true crime and writings on police procedure to science fiction to cooking to Texas history. The author of more than twenty books, he is a frequent guest at horror and mystery conventions. Joe and his wife Tina have two lovely daughters and make their home in a little town just outside of San Antonio, where he pursues his passion for cooking and makes what some consider to be the finest batch of chili in Texas. You can keep up with all of Joe's latest releases by friending him on Facebook.

Michael McCarty has been a professional writer since 1983 and the author of over forty books of fiction and nonfiction, including *I Kissed A Ghoul, A Little Help From My Fiends, Dark Duets, Liquid Diet & Midnight*

Snack, *Monster Behind The Wheel* (co-written with Mark McLaughlin), *Dracula Transformed and Other Bloodthirsty Tales* (also with Mark McLaughlin), the vampire Bloodless series: *Bloodless*, *Bloodlust*, and *Bloodline* (co-written with Jody LaGreca). He is a five-time Bram Stoker Finalist and in 2008 won the David R. Collins' Literary Achievement Award from the Midwest Writing Center.

He also author of the mega book of interviews *Modern Mythmakers: 35 Interviews With Horror And Science Fiction Writers And Filmmakers*, which features interviews with Ray Bradbury, Dean Koontz, John Carpenter, Richard Matheson, Elvria, Linnea Quigley, John Saul, Joe McKinney, and many more.

Michael McCarty lives in Rock Island, Illinois with his wife Cindy and pet rabbit Latte and can be reached: Twitter as michaelmccarty6.

His blog site is at: http://monstermikeyaauthor.wordpress.com

Facebook! Like him on his official page: http://www.facebook.com/michaelmccarty.horror. Or snail mail him at:

Michael McCarty
Fan Mail
P.O. Box 4441
Rock Island, IL 61204-4441

And check out these other novellas from

Death awaits you. Tim Ritter has just a few months left. At least that's what the doctors have told him.

But then he's been offered a second chance at life — and love. For a price. But is the price too high? The sacrifice too great?

Find out one man's answer to those questions in Dan Foley's *Gypsy*

.

It all started with the sibilant, unintelligible whispering and the movement of shadows within shadows. For Dennis Parkes, it was a sign of his worsening mental health. That is, until the day it spoke clearly and told him what it wanted.

Elsewhere in town, two amateur ghost hunters unearth what is believed to be *Gjallarbru*, a mythological bridge that connects the worlds of the living and the dead.

The dead are looking to cross over, as is the demon guardian, a guardian that has a craving for human flesh. As the veil between worlds weakens and darkness spreads over Ottmor Wood and the surrounding area, it's up to a group of friends to save their town, but are they enough? They have to be—because if they fail, the darkness will continue to spread, devouring everything in its path until there's nothing left to consume.

A lost child.

A marriage shattered beyond repair?

John Baxter doesn't think so, which is why he has planned this weekend getaway with his wife. He expected a lot of shouting, a lot of tears, but in the end, he hoped to have a stronger foundation upon which they could start rebuilding what they had once had.

What he wasn't expecting was the home invasion…

…and the hell that awaited them beneath the rented cabin.

"I killed my parents when I was thirteen years old."

And now, with the murder of Missy Blake twenty-two years later, it's time for Jack Greene to finish what he started.

When the co-ed's mutilated body is found, the police are clueless, but Jack knows what killed the pretty college student; he's been hunting it for years. The hunt has been going on for too long, though, and Jack wants to end it, but he can't do it alone. The local police aren't equipped to handle the monster in their midst, so Jack recruits Major Kelly Langston, and together they set out to rid the world of this murdering creature once and for all.